REA

ALLEN COUNTY PUBLIC LIBRARY

P9-AFS-033

"We'll get married as soon as we can."

"It's customary to ask a woman if she wants to get married. Not tell her."

"These are exceptional circumstances."

Her temper rose one notch. "I don't want to get married. Don't take it personally, Travis, it wouldn't matter who you were. The answer's no."

"You don't get it, do you? You're not being given a choice. I'll get a special license, probably next week."

"You don't love me," Julie said in a stony voice.

"We mean something to each other— you know that as well as I do. We'll build on that, Julie. There's something elemental between us," he said ruthlessly, raising one hand and running it down the side of her face to the hollow at the base of her throat, where her pulse quickened in spite of herself. "Don't bother denying it."

"You can't base a marriage on passion!"

"There are a lot worse things to base it on."

ROMANCE

This book is Part One in an exciting new duet

MILLNAIRE MARRIAGES

from talented Harlequin Presents® author

Sandra Field!

Book One—
The Millionaire's Marriage Demand
Meet Travis Strathern and Julie Renshaw—
and bear witness to the explosive chemistry
between them that has dramatic consequences!

And don't miss Book Two—
The Tycoon's Virgin Bride
Travis's sister Jenessa Strathern once had a
mammoth crush on Travis's best friend,
Bryce Laribee. Now, years later, she meets
Bryce again—and this time the
attraction is mutual!

Look for *The Tycoon's Virgin Bride*,
#2401, June 2004

Sandra Field

THE MILLIONAIRE'S MARRIAGE DEMAND

MILLIONAIRE
MARRIAGES

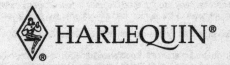

HARLEQUIN®

TORONTO • NEW YORK • LONDON
AMSTERDAM • PARIS • SYDNEY • HAMBURG
STOCKHOLM • ATHENS • TOKYO • MILAN • MADRID
PRAGUE • WARSAW • BUDAPEST • AUCKLAND

If you purchased this book without a cover you should be aware
that this book is stolen property. It was reported as "unsold and
destroyed" to the publisher, and neither the author nor the
publisher has received any payment for this "stripped book."

ISBN 0-373-12395-7

THE MILLIONAIRE'S MARRIAGE DEMAND

First North American Publication 2004.

Copyright © 2003 by Sandra Field.

All rights reserved. Except for use in any review, the reproduction or
utilization of this work in whole or in part in any form by any electronic,
mechanical or other means, now known or hereafter invented, including
xerography, photocopying and recording, or in any information storage
or retrieval system, is forbidden without the written permission of the
publisher, Harlequin Enterprises Limited, 225 Duncan Mill Road,
Don Mills, Ontario, Canada M3B 3K9.

All characters in this book have no existence outside the imagination of
the author and have no relation whatsoever to anyone bearing the same
name or names. They are not even distantly inspired by any individual
known or unknown to the author, and all incidents are pure invention.

This edition published by arrangement with Harlequin Books S.A.

® and TM are trademarks of the publisher. Trademarks indicated with
® are registered in the United States Patent and Trademark Office, the
Canadian Trade Marks Office and in other countries.

Visit us at www.eHarlequin.com

Printed in U.S.A.

CHAPTER ONE

SHE had the place to herself.

Heaven, Julie thought blissfully. The rocks and salt spray of the coastline where she'd grown up were what she missed most of all when she was overseas.

The tide was lapping at the wharf. She slipped her feet out of her sandals and with scant regard for her pretty summer dress sat down on the rough wood, dangling her legs over the edge. A wave grabbed at her bare toes. She gave a laugh of mingled shock and dismay; the water was icy cold.

What did she expect? After all, this was Maine and it was still June. She splashed her feet vigorously, watching how the golden light of early evening tangled itself in the foam. She was home again. Temporarily, to be sure, and not for the happiest of reasons. But home, nevertheless.

The wharf was at the end of a dirt road. To her ears wafted the sigh of wind through the pines and the chirping of sparrows in the underbrush; overlying everything was the steady hiss of surf against the shore of the nearest island.

Her destination was further out. She was spending the weekend on Manatuck Island, owned by Charles Strathern, whose son Brent had invited her to Charles's sixtieth birthday party tomorrow.

She'd been late leaving work this afternoon. By the time she'd driven from her apartment in Portland to this isolated shoreline, she'd missed the launch that was to have taken her and some of the caterers to the party. Now the launch had to make a return trip just for her.

She should be feeling guilty. But she wasn't. She splashed her feet again, hoping Charles Strathern had a heated swimming pool at Castlereigh, his estate on Manatuck. One thing Brent had made clear was that his father was very rich; the inference being that Brent, also, was more than comfortably off.

Julie sighed. Brent was handsome, charming and out for a good time. This meant, no doubt, that sooner or later she'd be fighting him off. Her spirit of adventure, that had caused her to live for the last few years in faraway places not always known for comfort or safety, didn't extend to sex. Or marriage, for that matter.

But for the space of a weekend, surrounded by Brent's family, she'd be safe enough.

Abruptly she turned her head, straining her ears. What had she just heard? A vehicle coming down the road? She didn't want company. Not right now. Oliver, captain of the launch, had been quite explicit that she was the only guest expected this Friday evening.

The unmistakable crunch of tires on gravel grew louder and louder. Julie scowled at the gold-tinted trees, inwardly urging the unknown interloper to stop at the last cottage a quarter of a mile from the wharf. To stop anywhere but here.

To leave her alone.

As the tires of his sleek black Porsche skidded in the gravel, Travis eased his foot off the accelerator. He was driving too fast. Partly, of course, because he was later than he'd wanted to be. He'd been doing fine until that emergency in intensive care, which had ended very satisfactorily for the patient but had put him way behind schedule.

Lateness wasn't the only reason he was driving fast. Gut-wrenching anxiety was the other reason. His lips stretched in a humorless smile. On a beautiful Friday evening in

June, when he could have been sailing on Penobscot Bay or going to the local opera with that nurse with the come-hither eyes, he was traveling to the one place in the world where he was guaranteed to get the cold shoulder.

Another quarter mile to the wharf. He'd use the phone on the dock there, contact Oliver and ask for the launch to be sent over. Once he was on the island, they couldn't very well send him back. Or if they tried, he'd put up one hell of a fight.

Through the open window he caught the scent of spruce resin mixed with the sharp tang of the ocean; he breathed deeply, filling his lungs, and for an instant was a little boy again, roaming the cliffs and rocky shoreline of Manatuck Island. Happy. Secure. With no inkling of what was to come.

It wasn't just the family he was returning to. It was the island as well. Of the two, he wasn't sure which had the greater potential for damage.

Probably the island.

Insanity to come back. Pure insanity.

The car swung around the last corner, and from the rise Travis saw the bay spread in front of him, its velvet-green islands sprinkling the deep blue waters, foam edging them like white ruffs. His throat tightened. One reason he'd driven himself so hard the last few years was to bury the blend of yearning and emptiness that was popularly called homesickness.

He jammed his foot on the brake. Someone was sitting on the wharf.

His gaze narrowed. Was it a teenager from one of the cottages up the road? Dammit, he didn't need company. If there was one time in his life he needed to be alone, it was right now, while he was waiting for the launch.

It wasn't a kid. It was a woman. She must be the driver

of the blue car that was parked by the side of the road above the wharf.

Travis swung the wheel, his tires grabbing at the gravel, and parked behind the blue sedan. It had a rental sign on the back bumper, he noticed absently. He got out of his car, slammed the door and strode down the slope toward the dock; as he did so, the woman stood up.

He'd get rid of her as fast as he could and then he'd contact Oliver.

Because the sun was behind him, she was bathed in soft light. His footsteps slowed. How could he ever have mistaken her for a young girl? Her flowered dress was full-skirted with a bodice that clung to her breasts and bared her shoulders and arms; her ankles and feet were soaking wet. Her hair was cut short, a gleaming dark cap that emphasized the slim line of her throat and her winged brows.

She was exquisitely, unbelievably beautiful.

She also, he realized, looked as displeased to see him as he'd been to see her. She said coolly, taking the initiative in a way that irked him, "Hello. Are you lost?" Giving him a quick survey that no doubt took in all six feet of him in his faded jeans and casual open-necked shirt, she added politely, "The road, as you see, comes to an end here. Perhaps you were looking for Bartlett Cove? The turnoff's about a half a mile back."

"No," Travis said brusquely, "I'm not lost—but you're trespassing. This wharf is on private property. It belongs to the owner of Manatuck Island."

"That's where I'm going."

"Oh? The party's not until tomorrow—did you get the timing wrong?"

"No, I didn't," she replied crisply.

His eyes clashed with her green ones. They couldn't really be that color, he thought. Eyes of a deep true green were very rare, and made comparisons with emeralds inevitable. Hers, at the moment, certainly looked as unyielding as emeralds. She was several inches shorter than he; why, when his normal fancy was for laughing blondes who were nearly his height, was he lusting after a brunette who looked about as warm as the ocean in January?

Light played across her high cheekbones, making him itch to stroke them; it took an actual physical effort to keep his hands at his sides. And all the while he was forcing himself to keep his gaze well above the entrancing shadow of her cleavage. What the devil was wrong with him?

Think, Travis. Use your much-vaunted brains. "Let me guess," he said softly. "You're arriving early on the island because you're Brent's date."

She bit one delectable lip. "How did you know?"

"Brent's always had a weakness for females with great bodies and more than passably pretty faces."

"When you've just complimented me twice over, why do I feel as though I've been thoroughly insulted?"

The wind suddenly seized her skirt, flattening it to her legs, then tugging it free to briefly bare her thighs. As she clutched at the brilliantly flowered fabric, thrusting it down to cover herself, Travis said hoarsely, "Your eyes—you must be wearing colored contacts?"

He'd had no intention of asking anything so personal; and was nevertheless furious when she disregarded his question. "Are you going to Manatuck as well?" she said bluntly.

"I am."

"And whose date are you?"

"Oh, I'm on my own," Travis said, giving her a smile that in no way touched his eyes. Eyes that could look through you as though you weren't there, Julie thought edgily, and heard him add, "I don't belong to anyone, it's against my principles."

"A principle I happen to share."

"I doubt that. Not if you're Brent's date."

The slight emphasis he put on the word *date* brought a flush to her cheeks. "His date is precisely—" she began, then broke off. Why was she defending her morals to a complete stranger?

He gave a short laugh. "I'm glad you didn't bother finishing your sentence. Brent's reputation precedes him."

"I won't ask if you're a friend of his. Obviously you're not."

"You got that right."

There was a depth of bitterness to his words that shocked Julie; she was suddenly aware of how tightly strung he was. As though he could explode any moment, she thought uneasily, and for the first time wished the wharf wasn't quite so isolated. Not another person in sight, and the nearest house a quarter of a mile up the road.

Normally she wasn't easily scared. She'd had too many close calls for that, too many times when she'd had to depend on her own resourcefulness to get her out of threatening situations. And this was Maine. Not Lima, or Dares-Salaam, or Calcutta.

When he'd walked down the slope toward her, he'd moved with the unconscious grace of the tiger she'd been lucky enough to sight in the mangrove swamps of West Bengal. Tigers might be graceful. They were also dangerous and had very sharp teeth.

Get a grip, Julie scolded herself. She had a trick or two up her sleeve when it came to self-defense. And so what if he was the kind of man who'd guarantee that any woman worthy of the name would be chomping at the bit? She said with a valiant attempt at friendliness, holding out her hand, "My name's Julie Renshaw."

With huge reluctance Travis clasped her hand, then dropped it as fast as he decently could. "Travis Strathern," he said.

She frowned. "Are you a cousin of Brent's?"

"No."

She flushed again at a reply whose brevity verged on rudeness. "Let me be honest," she said pleasantly. "I was really enjoying being alone until you came along, and it's pretty clear you're not craving my company. But we have to wait here for the launch and share the trip to the island. Couldn't we at least talk about the weather? Which, you must admit, is perfectly glorious."

Travis was known in some circles as a diplomat for his ability to smooth ruffled feathers under difficult circumstances; why had this ability been turned on its head by a pair of emerald eyes? He said incautiously, "If you think sunset's beautiful, wait until you see the sun rise through a mist lying low on the water..."

For a moment his gaze was lost in the past. Julie said curiously, "You've obviously been here before. If your last name's Strathern, I'm surprised they don't know you're coming—Oliver said I was the only guest arriving today."

They didn't know he was coming because he hadn't told them. Simple. Restlessly moving his shoulders, Travis said, "There must have been a mix-up."

He was, Julie thought, a very bad liar. But why would he bother lying to a complete stranger? Intent upon learning more about him, she said easily, "Have you visited Manatuck often?

"Not for years," he said shortly. "How did you meet Brent?"

"Through mutual friends. We've only had a couple of dates. But I've always wanted to stay on one of the islands, so I must admit I jumped at the chance of this weekend."

To his horror, Travis heard himself say, "So you're not Brent's lover?"

His question hung in the air. Julie said coolly, "You didn't mean to ask that, did you?"

She was much too astute for his own liking. "You're right—it was the wrong question," he said. "I should have asked if your eyes are really that green?"

If her eyes were green, Julie thought furiously, his were a startling blue. Yet close up, they yielded as little information about what lay below the surface as did the ocean. "Why do you care what color my eyes are?"

"Put it down to idle curiosity."

"I don't think anything's idle where you're concerned," she said dryly. "So if you're not Brent's cousin, who are you?"

His eyes narrowed. "What if I'm his elder brother?"

"What if the launch is docking right now?" she replied with gentle mockery. "He's never mentioned a brother to me."

"I'm sure he hasn't. What if you tell me the real color of your eyes?"

Thoughtfully Julie gazed up at him. She was realistic enough to know that her eyes were her best feature. Her creamy skin she was apt to curse in these days of high UV and sunscreen; her body had gotten her into hot water too many times to be considered a desirable asset. As for her hair, she'd cut it short several years ago, partly because Africa and India were hot countries, partly because she'd read somewhere that waist-length hair turned men into lustful idiots. Quite suddenly she began to laugh. "I'm not wearing contacts at all, bright green or otherwise—I have twenty-twenty vision. Do you want to know something else? My mother always said I was stubborn. But compared to you, I'm a rank amateur."

Although his own smile was reluctant, it changed his face immeasurably. The strong nose, firmly carved lips and hewn chin were still the same, as was the unruly hair, so dark as to be almost black; but the smile brought his features to life in a way that was wholly masculine and incredibly, compellingly sexy. Male energy, Julie thought dazedly, that's what powers him. Forceful, formidable and hugely charismatic energy. It enveloped her, almost as if he'd put his arms around her.

She took an unconscious step backward, saying breathlessly, "I've met a lot of men the last few years, many of them very attractive. But you, I have to say, take the cake."

His lashes flickered. Then he said ironically, "Good line. Now are you going to ask for my phone number? Brent won't like that."

"Don't tell me you're not fighting the women off. Because I won't believe you."

"Yeah," he drawled, "I fight 'em off. Like I said, I don't belong to anyone."

"Neither do I," she said softly. "And that includes Brent."

A flicker of rage removed any vestige of Travis's smile; Brent, unless Travis was very much mistaken, was the one who'd sealed his exile from Manatuck and from his father all those years ago. Was that why he couldn't bear the thought of Julie Renshaw as his brother's lover? But he'd only just met the woman. Why should he care what she did, or with whom? "Let me give you a word of advice," he said curtly. "Keep your distance from Brent this weekend. For your own good."

She blinked. "You hate him, don't you?" she said slowly.

"No! But I wouldn't want to see you out of your depth."

Too late, she thought with a flash of humor. Ten minutes of Travis's company and she was seriously out of her depth. She said, "I'm not going to—oh, there's the launch."

A sleek powerboat had just appeared from behind the nearest island. Travis's head swung around, his whole body taut with tension. Julie gaped up at him, quite sure he'd instantly and completely forgotten her presence. It was as though he were steeling himself for an ordeal, she thought wildly. As though whatever had brought him here would require all the courage and endurance he possessed.

He possessed a good deal. Intuitively she knew that.

Her gaze dropped. His fists were clenched at his sides, the knuckles white. With a compassion that had gotten her into trouble before, she rested a hand on his bare arm. "There's something really wrong here, isn't there?" she said. "Won't you tell me what it is? Maybe I can help."

Travis dragged his eyes away from the launch: the same launch on which, at the age of sixteen, he'd fled the island. He said with icy precision, "Why don't you mind your own business?"

She flinched, snatching her hand back. "Fine. Forget I asked."

In a whirl of skirts she ran away from him, along the length of the wharf and up the slope, her sandals scrabbling in the loose dirt. Once she reached her vehicle, she unlocked the trunk and took out a bag. Then she leaned against the side of the car, ostentatiously staring into the woods as though the pine trees were the most fascinating sight she'd ever seen.

Travis's jaw tightened. He didn't need her help. He didn't need anyone's. Ever since he'd first been banished from the island at the age of six, he'd managed on his own. And no woman, no matter how beautiful, was going to change that.

CHAPTER TWO

MOODILY Travis stared out to sea, where the setting sun was glancing off the polished bow of the launch. Unimaginatively, she was named *Manatuck,* after the island. A boat named after a woman was not for Charles; despite his two marriages, Charles Strathern didn't have much use for women.

Even less use for his elder son.

Or for his only daughter. Travis already knew that Jenessa wouldn't be on Manatuck for her father's birthday.

The launch was close enough that he could see Oliver's stout figure at the wheel; the bow wave curved backward in two white arcs. Slowly Travis turned and walked up the slope. He had to pass Julie's car to get to his. "Time to go down to the wharf," he said.

She nodded and headed down the hill. Her hips swung gracefully; her narrow shoulders filled him with passionate yearning. For what? For Brent's leftovers?

It was eighteen years since he'd laid eyes on Brent. Twice, in the early years, he'd made an effort to see his brother. But both times Brent had canceled their meeting at the last minute, and so Travis had stopped trying. Through mutual acquaintances he'd heard news over the years, mostly about Brent's profligate spending and strings of women.

Of which Julie Renshaw was the latest.

Cursing under his breath, Travis hefted his bag from the back seat. He dumped it on the wharf a few moments later and stationed himself by the rubber tires tied to the pilings to protect *Manatuck's* hull. Oliver cut the engine and with

15

a grappling hook latched onto one of the metal rungs bolted to the wharf. Then he looked up at the tall, dark-haired man on the dock. "Master Travis? Is that really you?"

The old name took Travis aback. He said, emotion roughening his voice, "Oliver...how are you? It's great to see you. But none of that master stuff—Travis is good enough."

"They didn't tell me you were coming," Oliver said gruffly, shoving his greasy cap further back on his head. "Darned if it's not good to see you, boy."

Oliver was almost bald, Travis noticed, and must have gained thirty pounds in the intervening years. "They don't know I'm coming—it's a surprise," he said dryly. "Isn't that the same shirt you were wearing the day I left?"

Oliver glanced down dubiously. "Can't be. Would have wore out by now. Looks like I spilled my dinner on it, though."

Forgetting his tension in a surge of affection, Travis said, "*Manatuck* looks good." The decks were shiny, the brass polished to a high luster, and the paintwork immaculate.

"She's aging better than I am," Oliver said. "Come on aboard, it'll be like old times."

No, it won't, Travis thought. You can't go back, he'd learned that the hard way. He said, indicating the woman standing silently beside him, "This is Julie Renshaw. Brent's date."

"Ah, yes," Oliver said, his faded blue eyes assessing her shrewdly. "Hand her bag down, Mr. Travis, and we'll get going. The tide'll be turning soon, and I'd just as soon be clear of the channel."

Julie picked up her bag. "I can manage," she announced, and passed it down to Oliver. Then she clambered down the metal rungs and jumped lightly onto the deck. "Hi, Oliver...I'm pleased to meet you."

Oliver grinned, baring the gap in his teeth that had been

there for as long as Travis could remember. "Master Brent arrived yesterday," he said. "Aren't you the pretty one, now."

Julie blushed. "Thank you."

Travis had also descended the ladder. The deck swayed gently beneath his feet. As Oliver dropped the grappling hook, Travis pushed off; with a sweet purr of her engines, *Manatuck* left the dock. Julie had stationed herself against the railing, where she could see where they were headed, but also keep Travis and Oliver in view. If Oliver liked Travis, then Travis couldn't be all bad, she thought. But there was a mystery attached to his return; the family didn't know about it, and she'd have sworn when she'd asked Brent about any siblings, he'd said no.

It looked like her weekend was shaping up to be more interesting than she'd expected. Rather too interesting. Travis had planted his feet on the deck, the wind ruffling his thick hair; his physique, broad-shouldered and slim-hipped, made her feel weak at the knees. Brent, technically the more handsome of the two men, and certainly friendlier, didn't have that effect at all.

Not that it mattered. She wasn't in the market for a lover, and definitely not for a husband.

The bay was choppy. She moved forward, clutching the railing, and wondered which of the islands was their destination. Fifteen minutes later, she was in no doubt. On the most rugged island in the bay, four stone turrets pierced the jagged outline of the spruce trees; Castlereigh, she thought with a quiver of inner laughter, and watched it come closer. A stone boathouse, twice the size of her parents' bungalow, anchored a long wharf which jutted out from the island; there was also a raked sand beach, and a vast expanse of manicured lawn.

Skillfully Oliver steered the launch to nudge the dock; Travis jumped ashore and fastened the lines. Then he reached down a hand to Julie. His face was inscrutable; his eyes didn't meet hers.

He lifted her to the dock as easily as if she were a child. Oliver slung their bags up. "See you tomorrow, Mr. Travis. Right glad you're back where you belong."

Although Travis had no idea where he belonged, he was almost sure it wasn't here. "Thanks, Oliver," he said, and picked up the two bags. "Let's go," he said to Julie.

He was striding up a long wooden stairway as though pursued by the hounds of hell. She jogged after him, past a thicket of rhododendrons and azaleas, followed by an enormous formal rose garden that would have graced the grounds of Versailles but was definitely out of place here. Then they rounded a copse of birch trees and she stopped dead in her tracks. "Well," she said inadequately.

For a moment Travis stopped, too. "It does kind of take your breath away, doesn't it?" he said wryly.

An array of crenellations, archways, porticos and buttresses was crowned by the four soaring turrets she'd seen from the launch. There was even a partial moat. She said faintly, "It's certainly imposing."

"It's a godawful monument to the triumph of money and egotism over taste," Travis said succinctly. "And you've only seen the outside."

"You mean there's more?"

"All that the almighty dollar can buy."

He looked fractionally less tense, Julie was glad to see. Although why his emotional state should matter to her, she didn't have a clue. He hadn't exactly been friendly to her; she'd better keep that in mind. "Is there a front door?" she asked. "Shouldn't I be mounted on a snow-white charger?"

"A suit of armor's not a bad idea," he said with a touch of grimness. "Follow me."

A massive bell pull dangled by twin doors that were

ornately spiked with wrought iron. Travis pulled the bell and pushed one door open. An aged butler was crossing the entrance hall. "Master Travis," he said, clutching his tailored black jacket in the vicinity of his heart. "Oh, Master Travis...how wonderful to see you, sir. It's been a long time."

"Hello, Bertram," Travis said, shaking the old man's hand. "Thought I'd surprise the family. How's your family, by the way?"

"Very well indeed. Peg will be so happy to know you're here. Cocktails are being served in the drawing room, sir. Shall I announce you?"

"Why don't you do that? This is Julie Renshaw, Brent's date."

Bertram gave her a courtly nod. In a procession of three they marched past a bloodthirsty display of medieval weapons, then down an imposing corridor checkered with portraits; not one of the painted faces, Julie noticed, looked at all happy to be hanging on the walls of Castlereigh. Travis didn't look very happy to be here, either.

As Bertram ushered them through a wide doorway, Travis took her by the hand. His fingers were cold; not for anything would she have let go of them. Bertram quavered, "Miss Julie Renshaw and Mr. Travis Strathern."

Three people were seated on overstuffed leather chesterfields in a room that dwarfed them with its dimensions. Quantities of marble and velvet, and carpets as big as playing fields were Julie's first impressions; her second the reaction of each of the three people to Travis's presence.

Brent leaped to his feet, turning to face the door. Hatred, raw and implacable, scored his face. He looked so unlike his usual handsome, carefree self that the hair rose on the back of Julie's neck. The older man, who must be Charles Strathern, looked terrified out of his wits; while the woman, impeccably dressed in linen and pearls, projected a well-bred mixture of dismay and distaste. Brent's stepmother, Julie decided, and watched as polite masks replaced all these initial, instinctive reactions.

Then Brent walked over to her, the lamplight shining in his golden hair, his perfect teeth stretched in a smile she would have sworn was genuine. She hadn't imagined the hatred, though. She knew she hadn't. "Julie!" he said, taking her by the shoulders. "How lovely you look." Before she could duck, he kissed her hard and thoroughly on the mouth.

Squirming free of Brent, suppressing the instinct to wipe her mouth with the back of her hand, she sputtered, "Hello, Brent. Sorry I'm late. But luckily Travis and I were able to get the launch together."

"Ah yes…my long-lost brother," Brent said. "A surprise birthday present, Travis. Is that what you are?"

His hazel eyes were entirely unamused; he was balancing lightly on the balls of his feet. Travis said easily, "Yes, I thought I'd surprise you all."

"How gratifying to have had such instant success," Brent said smoothly. "Be sure and tell Dad he hasn't aged," he added, swinging around to include Charles in his brilliant smile.

Why had it never struck her before how aggressive that smile was? Julie wondered. Or was she simply seeing for the first time what lay beneath the charm? She hadn't liked being kissed by him. Hadn't liked it at all. By kissing her, Brent had been getting at Travis, she'd swear to it; in that sense, it had been nothing to do with her.

Charles Strathern stepped forward. He was a tall man with iron-grey hair rigidly combed across his scalp, his chin stubborn rather than strong; he was wearing a tailored business suit. If he had been frightened earlier, he now had himself firmly under control. Making no effort to hug his son, or even shake his hand, he looked Travis up and down. "You'll just have time to change for dinner."

"I'll have a Scotch on the rocks first," Travis said calmly, yet with a note in his voice that caused his father's eyes to drop.

"Fine," Charles said. "Help yourself. But kindly say hello to your stepmother."

"Corinne," Travis said, crossing the room with that economical grace Julie had noticed earlier. He bent and brushed her perfectly made-up cheek with his lips. "You look very well."

"Thank you, Travis," she said coolly, without reciprocating his gesture. "Get your drink and I'll ring for Bertram to set another place for dinner."

Brent pulled Julie forward. "Dad, Corinne, this is Julie Renshaw. Julie, my father Charles Strathern, and my stepmother, Corinne Strathern."

Julie shook hands, murmured the usual inanities, and was offered an array of drinks. She chose vodka and orange, and heard herself chatting on about the boat trip and the rose garden. Corinne offered her a tour of the garden in the morning, then Charles led her to the far wall to show her an oil painting of *Manatuck's* predecessor. Travis said nothing.

Half an hour later, having been shown to her room, Julie closed the door and leaned back against the panels. She had fifteen minutes until dinner. Her sole desire was to run down the slope and beg Oliver to take her back to the mainland. Pronto.

What on earth had Travis done to make his return so little a cause for rejoicing? While Oliver and Bertram had been genuinely pleased to see him, his family was acting as if a viper had dropped into their midst. No one had welcomed him, or asked him how he was. Or why he was back.

The other glaringly obvious question was why he'd left. Why, when, and how.

She could always ask. Right, she thought ironically. A sure way to commit social suicide.

Her bag had been unpacked, and her clothes pressed and hung in a cavernous walk-in cupboard. Quickly Julie showered and changed into white silk pants with a long tunic, jade earrings that she'd bought at a bazaar in Tanzania dangling from her lobes, and jade-green sandals on her feet. Makeup, a quick brush through her hair and she was ready.

It was going to be a long evening.

As she walked down the hallway toward the magnificent curved staircase, another door opened. Travis said, "Wait, Julie, we'll go down together. Otherwise you'll get lost."

She turned. He was wearing a dark grey suit with a thin-striped shirt and silk tie; but his hair was still unruly, and his eyes remained that burning and unrevealing blue. Her heart quickened. Had she called him attractive? What a wishy-washy word for a man who exuded such a powerful combination of intelligence, willpower and animal grace. A man who pulled her toward him with every breath he took.

Which certainly made him unique. Normally she was immune to sexy, charismatic men. Avoided them like the plague.

He stopped a foot away from her, giving her a leisurely survey. "Very elegant—less is always more, isn't it? Something neither Charles nor Corinne has ever learned."

"I'm to take that as a compliment?"

"Don't fish, Julie."

"How else am I to find out what you're thinking?"

"You can take it as read that you're the most beautiful woman I've ever seen."

Her jaw dropped inelegantly. *"Me?"*

"Come on—you've looked in the mirror."

"My mouth is too wide and my nose is off-center."

"Only slightly. I never did have much use for perfection." Deliberately he reached out and ran his finger across the curve of her cheekbone to the corner of her mouth, where it lingered for a moment. "I've been wanting to do that since we met," he said thickly.

Warm color flooded her cheeks. "Come off it. You wanted the wharf to yourself when we met," she retorted. "Which, after that scene in the drawing room, I can fully understand. So please don't pretend you were overcome by the sight of me."

"You need to know two things about me. I don't pretend. And I'm capable of holding more than one emotion at once."

Wasn't she the same? If fury and lust could be called emotions, she was certainly swamped by both right now. Not that she was going to tell him that. She said lamely, "We're going to be late for dinner. Punishable by confinement in the dungeon."

"In irons." Travis held out his arm. "Let's go."

It was a challenge. He was daring her, Brent's date, to walk into the dining room on his arm. "Don't use me to get at your younger brother," she flared.

"Don't drag me down to his level."

He was saying, indirectly, that he wanted to take her arm for his own sake. Subduing a treacherous thrill of pleasure, she said, "Does anyone ever win an argument with you?"

He said dryly, "I have a feeling you could."

"I wish I shared that feeling," she said, and slid her fingers through the crook of his elbow, searingly aware of the taut muscles of his forearm under the expensive cloth. "Why are you here, Travis?" she blurted.

He said flatly, "It's time I made peace with my father. His sixtieth birthday seemed as good a time as any to start."

She looked straight up at him. "If peace is what you want, wouldn't you have been better to let him know you were coming? He looked scared out of his wits when he saw you."

"So you noticed that as well." Travis frowned. "Anger I'd have understood. But not fear."

"What if he doesn't want to make peace with you?"

"Then I'll just have to find a way to make it happen, won't I? And don't ask why I left, because I won't tell you."

"Well, that's straightforward enough." She gave him an impish grin. "This conversation will, I'm sure, be the only real one of the whole evening."

"What would you do if I kissed you right now?"

She blinked, swallowing hard. "Scream for help? Haul you into the nearest bedroom? How do I know?"

"Then we'd better postpone it until we have the time to find out," Travis said, and set off down the corridor as imperturbably as if they'd been discussing the weather.

Julie scurried along beside him, her head buzzing with questions, her body, regrettably, aching with a hunger that had nothing to do with dinner. When would she ever learn to keep a guard on her tongue?

How could she have said that about hauling him into the nearest bedroom? She'd never hauled a man into a bedroom in her life; and she wasn't going to start with Travis Strathern.

CHAPTER THREE

DINNER was an interminable, exquisitely prepared meal during which Brent flirted with Julie unrelentingly, Corinne talked at great length about gardens of the eighteenth century, and Charles and Travis said very little. Julie did learn two things. Travis was a doctor, and he'd left home eighteen years ago.

It didn't seem like much for the better part of two long hours, every minute of which seethed with the undercurrents of things unsaid. Just like home, Julie thought with a touch of panic. When had her parents ever voiced an honest emotion or spoken out of a genuine need? Never. Excruciating politeness was the way they operated, too, just like the Stratherns. And it was from that deadly politeness that she herself had run away from home at the age of seventeen and a half.

By ten o'clock Julie had the beginnings of a headache, which she used as the excuse to beg off after-dinner drinks on the stone patio that led from the dining room. As Brent accompanied her to the dining-room doorway, she managed to turn her head so that his good-night kiss hit her cheek rather than her mouth. His fingers digging into her arm with punitive strength, he said in a voice laden with innuendo, ''Sleep well, darling.''

''Thank you...good night, everyone.''

She almost ran up the stairs to her room. Once inside, after a moment's thought, she locked the door, using the heavy brass key. Brent hadn't liked her entering the dining room arm in arm with Travis. Brent might possibly be planning a middle-of-the-night revenge. Well, she'd foiled that, she thought smugly, and stripped off her clothes.

Accepting Brent's invitation for the weekend hadn't been the smartest move of her life. But she'd had two fun-filled dates with him, the first a seafood dinner followed by a movie, the other sailing with two other couples in the bay; so it had seemed safe enough to come to Manatuck. It might well have been safe if only Travis hadn't shown up.

Travis wasn't safe.

She pulled on her nightgown and prowled around the room, picking up some of the heavy marble statuettes and putting them down again. Why was a bedroom in a fake medieval castle decorated with naked Greek goddesses, an Elizabethan four-poster and imitation Louis XIV chairs? Travis was right. Too much hard cash and too little restraint.

She was thinking about Travis again. As the soft fabric of her gown brushed her nipples, she shivered, wondering what it would be like were he to touch her breasts. His fingers were long and lean, and his strength and lightning-swift reactions she'd already experienced. When had she ever felt such helpless and overwhelming hunger for a man's touch?

Never. She'd been too busy keeping each and every man she met at a distance. So why didn't that work with Travis?

With an impatient sigh, Julie put a simpering marble nymph back on the mantel of the Victorian tile fireplace. She'd eaten too much, that was her problem; and her brain was as restless as a squirrel in a cage. She carefully opened the glass doors to the balcony, which was screened with lush Virginia creeper and scented with the climbing roses espaliered below her window. What had Corinne called them? Evangeline?

The soft swish of waves on the shore soothed her ears; a delicate crescent moon was couched on an array of sparkling stars. And then she heard something else: the scrape of chairs on flagstone, and voices. All too familiar voices coming from the patio two stories down. Her body tensed.

"I fail to understand why you didn't warn us you were coming," Charles said furiously.

"Because I knew you'd tell me to stay away," Travis said.

"You'd have been right. Don't you realize that tomorrow night all my friends will be here? That we'll have to make up some kind of story to account for your presence?"

"Tell them the truth, Dad. That I've come home to make peace with you."

"You must see that your father couldn't possibly do that," Corinne interposed. "You abandoned us all eighteen years ago, Travis. You can't expect to walk in as though nothing's happened."

"Abandonment can go two ways, Corinne."

"Nonsense! You always had a home here."

"The minute my mother died, I was parceled off to boarding school. I wasn't even allowed back on the island the first two summers."

"That was before my time," Corinne said fastidiously.

"Boarding school was the best place for you," Charles snapped. "You never liked the Boston house. And out here you were running wild. Spending day after day on the cliffs watching seagulls when you should have been playing football."

"Stick to the facts. You didn't want me around."

"Boarding school made a man out of you."

"Was that what it did? So why did you kick me out of the house when I turned sixteen?"

"You know the answer to that—you'd smeared my name in all the papers, made a laughingstock out of me. And then to cap it all you stole the family ring." Charles's voice roughened. "Where is that ring, Travis? Did you sell it?"

"I never took it."

"It disappeared the same night you did...I've never forgiven you for stealing it like a common thief."

"If you knew me at all, Dad, you'd know that I might stab you in the chest, but never in the back. It's not the way I operate."

Brent said smoothly, "So your opportune arrival this evening doesn't have anything to do with the lawyers who are going to rewrite Dad's will in the next couple of weeks?"

There was a small, deadly silence. Julie held herself painfully still, knowing she shouldn't be listening, afraid that if she retreated to her room, they'd hear her. "No," Travis rapped. "This is the first I've heard of it. I don't need Dad's money, I've got my own."

"What you earn as a doctor?" Brent mocked. "Come off it, brother dear—we're talking big bucks here."

"Are you forgetting I inherited my share of Grandad's money when I turned thirty? You'll do the same, Brent. Or can't you wait that long?"

Corinne said sharply, "Stop it, you two! This has gone on long enough. You've come back, Travis, but in view of all you've done, reconciliation is impossible. You must leave in the morning. I'll order the launch first thing after breakfast."

"No, Corinne," Travis said, so quietly Julie had to strain to hear him.

"Of course you must leave!" Charles blustered.

"I'll make that unanimous," Brent said lazily.

Travis said evenly, "I left when I was just a kid. Barely sixteen. I'm thirty-four now, and I've changed. I don't want your money, Dad, I never did. But I do want my family back. You back. It's that simple."

"You ran away," Charles fumed. "For six weeks we

didn't even know if you were alive or dead. And you took the ring with you.''

"I'm sorry I didn't get in touch. But I was young, and just as headstrong as my father. As for the ring, all I can say is that I never touched it. For heaven's sake, Dad, I knew what that ring meant to you.''

"You trashed me in the press.''

"You were hiring illegal immigrants in your factories and paying them a pittance,'' Travis said, exasperated. "I spoke to you about it, begged you to increase their wages and approach immigration so they could get their papers. But you refused. So yes, I went to the press. I didn't know what else to do.''

"You'd do it again, wouldn't you?''

"I'd find some other way of dealing with it now.''

"You haven't really changed,'' Charles said in a hard voice.

"The past is the past. Can't we let it go?''

"Corinne's right...you must leave in the morning.''

"Unless you're prepared to set Bertram and Oliver on me, I'm staying,'' Travis said with a lightness that didn't quite ring true.

A chair was pushed back. Corinne said briskly, "Why don't we all sleep on it? I'm sure in the morning you'll have reconsidered, Travis, and see our point of view. Are you coming, Charles? Bertram will clean up. Good night, Brent.''

"Good night, Dad,'' Travis said.

"Humph,'' said Charles. The patio door closed with a decisive click.

"In disgrace again, Travis,'' Brent said lightly. "Just like old times.''

"What did you do with the ring, Brent?''

Brent hesitated just too long. "Nothing!''

"Somebody took the ring, and it wasn't me. That leaves

you. Did you hide it somewhere? Come on, you were only ten. No one's going to hold it against you after all these years.''

"It won't wash, Travis. Why don't you just confess? Who knows, Dad might even forgive you.''

"He loved that ring. Tell me where it is.''

"Lay off," Brent said in a furious whisper. "And lay off Julie as well. She's my date, not yours.''

"I don't know Julie very well, but I do know one thing—she's got a mind of her own. Why don't we let her decide whose date she is?''

"Stay out of my way—I'm telling you!''

"I don't take orders kindly. Especially from you...good night, Brent.''

Again Julie heard the soft swish of the patio door. Then, making her jump, a glass suddenly shattered, as though Brent had hurled it against the stone wall. A chair clattered to the floor. Once again, the door clicked shut.

She took a long, shaky breath. How was she ever going to behave tomorrow as though ignorant of all she'd over-heard? No wonder eavesdropping wasn't recommended.

She now knew why Travis had left the island, and why he hadn't been welcomed home. After the public exposure of his father's labor practices and a stolen heirloom ring it was little wonder his family wasn't embracing him.

But her mind seethed with other images: a tousle-haired boy watching the gulls soar by the cliffs. The same boy exiled to boarding school and not allowed back to his island home for two long years. Tears pricked at the back of her eyes.

Oliver and Bertram, she'd be willing to bet, didn't believe Travis had stolen the family ring. But if he hadn't, who had? Brent?

She gave a heavy sigh. Bed. That's what she needed. Bed and a good night's sleep.

Would she wake in the morning to find that Travis had reconsidered? And once again had left the island?

Eventually Julie did fall asleep. She dreamed about Travis, first that they were driving full speed on a gravel road to an island where they would dig for hidden treasure, gold rings and rusty, iron-studded suits of armor; and then, abruptly, that they were making impassioned love on a blanket of roses called Evangeline. The dream slid into wakefulness, into a flicker of candlelight and a man's hand fumbling for her breast. Travis, she thought in a flood of delight, and turned to face him, opening her eyes.

Travis didn't have blond hair.

It wasn't Travis. It was Brent.

She shoved herself backward in the bed, hit her wrist on one of the four posts and tumbled off the edge in a welter of sheets. Frantically she struggled to extricate herself. "For Pete's sake, Julie," Brent hissed, "what are you trying to do? Wake the entire household?"

She tugged at her nightgown, covering her breasts. "Get out of here—right now."

He rolled off the other side of the bed as she scrambled to her feet; he was bare-chested, she noticed with the small part of her brain that appeared to be working. "How did you get in?" she demanded. "I locked the door."

"Bertram keeps a set of spare keys in the pantry."

"I locked it for a reason," she blazed; after all the stresses of the evening before, it felt very liberating to lose her temper. "I'm not your lover. I never have been and I never will be."

"You're old enough to know the score, Julie. Why do you think I invited you here for the weekend?"

Travis's reasoning exactly. She told the exact truth. "Because I'd told you how homesick I get for the ocean."

"Sure," he jeered, "your little miss naive act."

"It's no act. I don't do casual sex. Maybe you should have checked that out before inviting me out here."

"So you're all come-on and no delivery."

In a cold fury she said, "I haven't encouraged you in any way to think that I'd get into bed with you."

"That dress you had on when you got here, all bare shoulders and cleavage—you don't call that a come-on?"

"It's a perfectly ordinary sundress and why are we standing here in the middle of the night discussing my wardrobe?" She grabbed the nearest marble statue, a particularly nubile Aphrodite. "Get out of here, Brent, or I'll scream the place down. I have very good lungs, believe me."

"So is it Travis you want?"

"I don't want either one of you! Head for the door."

For a moment he hesitated, the muscles bunched in his arms. She tensed, wondering if she'd have the nerve to hit him with a solid marble goddess; to her great relief, he took a couple of steps away from the bed. "What a little Puritan you are."

"Out," she said.

He sauntered over to the chair, picked up his shirt and crossed the room. "Just stay out of my way for the rest of the weekend," he said.

"You haven't got a worry in the world." All she could think of was how he'd entered her room while she was asleep and watched her, leisurely taking off his shirt in the meantime. It made her feel dirty all over.

As the door closed softly behind him, Julie let out her breath in a ragged sigh. There was no point in locking it. Grunting with effort, she dragged the cedar chest from the foot of her bed until it was lodged against the panels, and sat down hard. Now that Brent was gone, she was trembling with delayed reaction.

She'd find Oliver in the morning and go back to the

mainland with him on his first crossing. She'd had her fill of the Strathern family. And that included Travis just as much as the rest of them.

She didn't need seducing, even in her dreams.

CHAPTER FOUR

TRAVIS was wide-awake at 5:00 a.m. He hadn't been given his old room up in the tower, but rather one of the guest suites. Another message that he wasn't welcome here, he thought with a wry twist of his lips. And another reason why he'd had one of the worst night's sleep in his life.

But not the main reason. Not if he were honest.

His room was down the hall from Julie's. He'd sat on a rock by the shore for a long time after that scene on the patio, then come up the back stairs to go to bed. In consequence, he'd had a ringside view of Brent leaving Julie's bedroom in the middle of the night. His brother's shirt had been casually looped over his arm, the night-lights gleaming on his bare chest.

Even now, several hours later, Travis's gut clenched at the memory. Julie had been lying to him all along. Swearing that she belonged to herself, not to Brent. It had been an act. An impressively credible one, moreover. Her big green eyes had been so full of sincerity, had met his so unflinchingly...but she'd been deceiving him from the beginning.

He sat up in bed, running his fingers through his hair. Twenty-four hours ago he hadn't even met Julie. Hadn't known she existed. So why did it matter so much that she'd lied to him?

The thought of her in Brent's arms, making love, was more than he could stomach. Jealousy, hot and lethal, surged through his veins. He wanted her for himself. Himself alone.

Not likely. If he didn't believe in casual sex, even less did he believe in sharing his lover with another man.

Particularly when the man was his brother.

Corinne was right, Travis thought sickly. There was no point in him staying here. Charles still resented him for going to the media, an action Travis had regretted as he'd aged and gathered experience; there must have been a better way of dealing with that situation. But he'd been young and hotheaded and deeply angry with the man who'd exiled a little boy from the island he'd loved, and so he'd acted without thought of the consequences.

What really hurt was that Charles still thought him capable of stealing the family ring.

He'd take Corinne's advice, and leave on the first boat this morning. Reconciliation was impossible, a pipe dream. He'd been a fool to come here, stirring up all the old animosities.

Restlessly Travis got up from the bed and stared out the window. The launch wouldn't be leaving for another four hours. He could at least walk along the cliffs to the lighthouse before he left. Feeling minimally better for this decision, Travis hauled on his jeans and a T-shirt, and padded down the corridor in his socked feet, his sneakers in his hand. He let himself out the west door, taking a deep breath of the cool morning air. The grass was wet with dew, the birds singing as though this was the first morning of creation. After doing up his laces, Travis set off.

It took a full five minutes to get clear of the painstakingly tended gardens and lawns, another five to cross the equally artful natural garden, the trees carefully placed, the stream rerouted beneath a whimsical bridge. But finally he reached the edge of the forest, and the track that he'd blazed himself many years ago. Although it had grown over considerably, it was still passable.

When a redstart flitted through the maples, he stopped to

admire its black and orange plumage. Next he startled a rabbit, then a red squirrel dropped a pinecone on his head. Laughing, he tossed it back up the tree. The squirrel scolded him indignantly; for the first time in hours, Travis felt like a human being. Shutting his mind to family and Julie alike, he strode on, feeling his muscles loosen and watching the rising sun spear through the thick spruce boughs.

A perfect day for his father's party. Even if he himself wouldn't be in attendance.

Fifteen minutes later Travis emerged at the brink of the granite cliffs on the offshore side of Manatuck. Bear Island, the next island beyond Manatuck, belonged to him, willed to him by his grandfather. It, too, was very beautiful.

He might just build a cabin on it. Use it as a getaway when his job got too much for him. If he placed the cabin carefully, he wouldn't even have to see Castlereigh.

He tramped along, gulls and kittiwakes swirling like tossed white papers over the turquoise sea. At the foot of the lighthouse that warned of the reefs further east, he threw himself down on the wet grass. How often had he lain here as a young boy, listening to the thunder of the surf?

He laced his fingers behind his head and closed his eyes. It wouldn't have to be a very big cabin. A wharf would be essential; but there was a perfect natural harbour at the southwest end of the island, so that wouldn't be a problem…mentally he started cataloging all the birdcalls he could hear, amused to discover that he hadn't lost his old talent. Gradually his mind quietened. He was almost asleep when a new noise startled him, the snapping of twigs along the path. Remembering that occasionally a deer would land on Manatuck after swimming the channel, Travis twisted over onto his stomach.

It wasn't a white-tailed deer that emerged into the clearing behind the lighthouse; it was Julie.

She was wearing bright pink shorts and a white shirt; she hadn't seen him. As Travis surged to his feet, he watched her whirl, as startled as any deer. "Travis, you frightened me—I wasn't expecting to see anyone." Then she smiled at him, a generous smile full of delight. "Isn't it a glorious morning?"

All the emotions of the last twelve hours coalesced into a flame of rage. Travis crossed the wet grass, standing very close to her. "I'm surprised you're up so early," he grated. "After making love to Brent half the night."

Her smile was wiped from her face; he could almost see her brain working. "You saw him leave my room," she said in an unreadable voice.

"Yes, I did. Not that you're sleeping with him, of course."

Refusing to drop her eyes, Julie said, "I didn't make love with Brent. Nor did I, in the literal sense of the words, sleep with him."

"Why don't you tell the truth for once?"

"Why don't you listen when I do?"

"I believe what I see. And what I saw was my brother leaving your room at two-thirty in the morning, in his bare feet and carrying his shirt over his arm."

"Too bad you hadn't seen me threatening him with a marble statue of Aphrodite and then dragging a cedar chest across the door so he couldn't get in again!"

"Didn't you like him as a lover?" Travis snarled.

Hands on her hips, she railed, "You listen to me—I locked my bedroom door last night when I went to bed because the thought crossed my mind that Brent might try some funny business in the middle of the night. But Bertram, bless his doddery old soul, keeps a spare set of keys in the pantry where everyone can help themselves. Did I know that? No, I did not!"

As she briefly paused for breath, Travis said nastily, "If

you had, you'd have done the cedar chest routine when you went to bed. I bet.''

As quickly as it had flared to life, Julie's temper died, leaving her with a horrible emptiness in her belly. She dropped her hands to her sides. "You won't believe me whatever I say, will you, Travis? You made your mind up about me the first moment you saw me on the wharf. Fine, believe what you like. See if I care.''

She sounded like a kid in kindergarten, she thought in despair, and pivoted so she could hurry back down the path. Anywhere, just as long as she could run from the contempt in Travis's face. Tears blurring her vision, she stumbled over a rock.

Travis grabbed her around the waist. She flailed out at him, striking him on the wrist. "Take your hands off me!''

Instead he pulled her to face him, lifted her chin and kissed her full on the mouth. For Julie, this was the last straw. She wrenched her mouth free, the tears now streaming down her cheeks. "*Don't!* You're no better than he is.''

Travis stared at her, appalled. She thought he was like Brent. That was what she was saying. According to her, first Brent had attacked her, and now he, Travis, was doing the same thing. Acting instinctively, he smoothed away the tears that were dribbling down to her chin. "Don't cry, Julie,'' he said in a raw voice. "Please don't cry.''

She pulled a crumpled tissue from her pocket and blew her nose. "I'm not crying,'' she said defiantly. "I never cry over men, they're not worth it.''

Her eyes were still shimmering with tears; he could feel them drying on his palm, in a way that seemed incredibly intimate. But before he could think of anything else to say, she hiccuped, "Do you know what was worst about last night? He let himself into my room while I was asleep and then he just sat there, watching me.'' Her breath caught on another sob. "I hate the thought of him doing that. Besides, I was d-dreaming about you."

"About me?" Travis repeated stupidly.

"Oh God, I shouldn't have told you that. My tongue's always running away with me, my mother says it's one of my worst faults and she's right. Forget I ever mentioned it. I'm going back to my room to pack, I'm going to eat a huge breakfast and then I'm going right back to the mainland with Oliver. I've had enough of you and your family and that horrible Disneyland heap of stone."

Travis said, a quiver of laughter in his voice, "I was planning to do exactly the same."

She gave him a look that was far from friendly. "You can go on a later boat. Not on mine."

"Surely there's room on the launch for both of us."

"There wouldn't be room on the *Titanic* for you and me. Besides, you came here to make peace with your father, that's what you told me. So do it. And good luck to you."

Travis said carefully, "So you didn't make love with Brent last night? You've never made love with him?"

"Two brilliant deductions. You can add something else. I never will make love with Brent."

Could he believe her? Going to her room in the dead of night would be the sort of stunt Brent would pull. Travis said sharply, "Did he hurt you?"

"He did not. Although I broke two fingernails on one corner of the cedar chest."

His breath escaped from his lungs in a small whoosh. But he had one more question. "What kind of dream was it? The one about me, I mean."

"Never you mind."

"Unprintable?"

Hurriedly she changed the subject. "Did you spend much time here as a boy?"

"Until I was six, yes," he said shortly. "Then I was sent to boarding school."

"Which, by the look of you, you hated."

"Yeah," he said dismissively. "Although later on I made a good friend there—we still keep in touch. Bryce was as big a rebel as I was." He gave a reminiscent smile. "Once we took all the masters' black gowns and draped them around the cows in a nearby field. They were Jersey cows, the ones with the big eyelashes, they looked very sweet. We nearly got expelled for that."

"I put banana peels in the church organ when I was nine. But I didn't get caught."

As mischief danced in her eyes, Travis laughed. "Does that mean you're smarter or sneakier?" Then, suddenly intent, he added, "Why don't you cry about men, Julie? And how many men are we talking about here?"

She put her head to one side, her amusement fading. "You and I are going our separate ways today. I don't really think my romantic past, such as it is, is any of your business."

"Where do you live?"

"Portland. For now."

"So do I. It's a small place—we'll probably bump into each other."

"I doubt it—I won't be there long."

She'd retreated from him in a way he couldn't fathom, and that at some deep level angered him intensely. "What are you running away from?"

"You're a fine one to talk. You're giving up on your father without a fight."

"You know nothing about my father and me. So lay off," Travis said softly.

She knew quite a bit; but she wasn't about to reveal she'd eavesdropped on an acrimonious family discussion. By the look of him, he'd bite her head off. She said flatly, "I'm going to walk back along the cliffs. Goodbye, Travis. It's been interesting meeting you."

Not so fast, he thought, and said with a lazy grin, "I'll stay for the party if you will."

"That's boarding school talk!"

"Scared to stay, Julie? Surely you're not scared of me?"

One of the several ways she'd rebelled against the sterility of her upbringing had been to accept any dare that came her way; she still had the scars where she'd fallen off the high brick wall that surrounded her elementary school. Hadn't every job she'd ever taken been a continuation of that dare?

Travis was just a man. She'd been exaggerating her response to him; she'd never had any trouble handling men before. And despite what she'd said to him about going back to the mainland, she was intensely curious to learn more about the Stratherns and their tangled family history. "If you stay, you have to make an effort to reconcile with your father," she said, tossing her head.

"If you stay, you have to keep your distance from Brent."

"No problem," she said fervently.

"Done," Travis said, took her in his arms and kissed her.

He'd intended it as a joke, a way of sealing their bargain. But as her body stiffened in his embrace, her palms pushing against his chest, it very soon changed into something else. Fire streaking through his belly. A searching for a response he wanted more than he'd ever wanted anything before. He moved his lips over hers, one hand stroking her spine, the other moving lower to clasp her by the hips.

With a suddenness that jolted through his body, Julie kissed him back. The resistance melted from her frame; her hands moved up his shoulders to lace themselves behind his head, her fingers tangling in his hair. In a surge of heat he felt the softness of her breasts against his chest, and deepened his kiss, easing her lips apart, drinking deeply of their sweetness.

His groin hardened. But instead of moving away, she leaned into him, her hips pressed to his. "Julie," he muttered, "beautiful Julie," and thrust with his tongue. His whole body was aflame with need. And what better place to make love with her than here, his favorite haunt since he was a small boy?

She was willing. He was in no doubt of that.

He fumbled for the hem of her shirt, easing his hand beneath it to find the silky smoothness of her back, the curved ridges of her ribs. With another of those disorienting jolts he realized she wasn't wearing a bra; as his fingers slid around her ribs to cup the soft swell of her breast, she whimpered with pleasure.

Her nipple hardened beneath his thumb. He plundered her mouth, desperate for her, and felt her tug his T-shirt free of his jeans. Then her palm glided from his navel up to the tangle of dark hair on his chest. He freed his mouth long enough to mutter, "We're wearing far too many clothes." Easing her away, he reached for the top button on her shirt. "I want to see you. All of you. Lie down with me, Julie..."

Her eyes were dazzled, her skin delicately flushed; her mouth was swollen from his kisses. He nibbled gently at her lower lip, murmuring between kisses, "I want you so much, you're so lovely, so generous." With a husky laugh he added, "But the buttons on your shirt are much too small...can you help me?"

Taking her consent as a given, he hauled his shirt over his head. She was standing very still, watching him, her eyes glued to the taut lines of his body. Her face convulsed, and briefly she pressed her hands to her cheeks. She looked stunned, he thought. Stunned and frightened out of her wits. Frightened? Of him? "You don't need—"

She said faintly, as though he hadn't spoken, "Travis, we can't! We can't make love like this. We don't know the first thing about each other, and all we've done is fight ever since we met." Her breath caught in a little sob. "It would be madness."

Her distress was all too evident; it was no act. Even so, he was almost sure that if he kissed her, he could change her mind. But did he want to make love with her and then have her regret it afterward? He said hoarsely, "Let me tell you this much—I've never wanted anyone the way I want you. And that's the God's truth."

She bit her lip. "You terrify me," she whispered. "You make me into a stranger, a woman I don't even know. I never behave like this. Never!"

The tumult in his body was slowly subsiding. Travis said roughly, "Stay, Julie. Stay the whole weekend. At least do that."

"I don't know. I just don't know!"

She was like a hare cornered by wolves, he thought, with the same desperate need for escape. He'd been a fool to kiss her so passionately, frightening her away.

What scared him was how little choice he'd had; how something about her called to him in the most primitive way possible. And explain that if you can, Travis Strathern.

He should be begging her to leave, not to stay. He had enough on his plate right now without adding to the mix a woman as complex and desirable as Julie.

"I've got to get out of here," she muttered. "I can find my own way back— I'll see you at breakfast."

In full view of the family. He said, making no attempt to hide his frustration, "I don't know the first thing about you—where you live in Portland, whether you're working there, where you're from."

She looked straight at him. "You know something about me I didn't even know myself," she whispered. Then, before he could respond, she'd turned and was running down the path. The shrubs closed over her passage, the leaves swaying and then still. As though he'd dreamed her, Travis thought. As though she didn't really exist.

CHAPTER FIVE

BY THE time Julie had crossed the ornately carved bridge over the stream, she was panting for breath. She'd run hard all the way from the cliffs; and it had helped her make up her mind. She'd go straight to her room to pack. Then she'd go in search of Oliver to find out what time he was leaving for the mainland; she could always tell Corinne and Charles that her headache was worse, not better.

Running away, Julie?

You're darn right, she thought, bursting out of the woods, then stopping dead in her tracks. Corinne, tastefully dressed in tailored trousers and a pale pink sweater, was clipping roses in the garden, laying them in a basket that could have come out of a Jane Austen novel. She raised her head when she saw Julie. "Good morning," she said cordially. "How are you feeling, Julie? Better, I gather?"

Julie swallowed a tremor of laughter. She could hardly say her headache was worse, not when she'd been pounding through the woods as though she were training for a marathon. "It's fine, thank you. What beautiful colors!"

"I want them for decorating the buffet table tonight." Corinne started naming the different varieties, giving Julie a brief history of each as she went. Julie listened with half her attention, wondering why Corinne couldn't be as interested in her stepson's welfare as she was in her roses. Then Corinne broke off to ask, "Have you seen Travis this morning by any chance?"

"He's out at the lighthouse."

"I should have guessed that's where he'd be." Rather too casually, Corinne added, "He did say last night that he may not stay for the party. Oliver could take him back around nine.''

Julie didn't know if Travis was going to stay. Even less did she know her own decision. She stared down at the petals of a rose called Ferdinand Pichard, its petals striped deep pink and white. Passion and purity, she thought, and forced down the memory of Travis's devastatingly passionate kisses, and her own equally ardent response.

Stay or go. Which was it to be?

"Are you sure you're all right?" Corinne asked.

"I'm fine." Julie gulped, and added impulsively, "I hope Travis will stay. He mentioned something about making peace with his father. Life's too short for families to be estranged, wouldn't you agree, Corinne?"

Corinne snipped off a spray of creamy floribundas. "Travis isn't easy to get along with. Nor do I want anything to spoil Charles's party—we've gone to far too much trouble and expense for that." Reaching for a delicate pale yellow rose centered with pink, she added, "Have you known Brent long?"

"Long enough," Julie said dryly, not really caring how Corinne interpreted that. "I'm going to have a shower, I'll see you at breakfast."

She marched across the grass. Huge tents with striped awnings were being erected near the main door; baskets of blue and pink hydrangeas flanked the stone walls. It would be a beautiful party, she thought irritably. Appearance over substance. Just like her entire life with her parents.

Would Travis stay? Or would he leave?

When Travis entered the dining room, where breakfast was always served buffet style on the vast mahogany sideboard, Charles and Corinne were already there. "Good morning," he said pleasantly. "No sign of Brent?"

"Brent rarely eats breakfast," Charles said shortly.

"Did you sleep well?" Corinne asked with punctilious good manners.

"About as badly as a man can sleep," Travis said. "I'm staying, Dad. I'll tell everyone tonight that I just got in from Angola, that's why they haven't seen me around. And before that it was Tanzania and Laos. Apart from anything else, it happens to be the truth."

"And when are you returning to Angola?" Charles rapped.

"I've taken over a private practice in Portland for the summer, because the resident doctor wanted to go to Scotland with his family. So I'll be heading out early in the fall. Although probably not back to Angola."

"All summer?" Charles croaked.

Travis's voice sharpened. "What's the matter?"

"You're spending the whole summer in Portland?"

"That's right." Trying to ignore the fact that his father looked aghast, Travis gave him a crooked smile. "Maybe you'll invite me out to the island in a couple of weeks, when we'll have more time to talk."

Charles took a big gulp of coffee. "I want to talk to you now, Travis. Or at least right after breakfast. Corinne, would you pass the marmalade, please?"

Travis poured a large glass of freshly squeezed orange juice. He had no idea what was going on. But at least Charles wanted to talk to him. That was a hopeful sign.

Why hadn't Julie arrived for breakfast? Had she already left? The launch had still been at the dock when he'd walked back from the lighthouse, and there'd been no sign of Oliver. How would he feel if he never saw her again?

Then footsteps tapped across the oak floor and Julie walked through the door. She was wearing her flowered sundress with scarlet flat-heeled sandals; her hair was damp from the shower. Travis's fingers tightened around his glass. What had happened out at the lighthouse had been no aberration; he wanted her now just as much as then.

With old-fashioned courtesy Charles got to his feet. "Good morning, Julie. Did you sleep well?"

"I woke up early," she said truthfully, "so I went out to the lighthouse." She smiled at Charles. "I can see why Travis loves Manatuck—it's so beautiful out there."

Travis swallowed a smile. Charles said manfully, "I'm glad you're having a good time. I hope you'll join me in a game of tennis later this morning?"

There was a fractional hesitation; Travis held his breath. Then Julie said, "That'd be lovely. Although I haven't played for quite a while."

She was staying. Travis turned back to the sideboard, staring at a platter of sliced fruit as if he'd never seen melons and strawberries before. So the die was cast. For the next twenty-four hours the two of them would be together on the island.

Julie started asking questions about the history of Manatuck, a subject dear to Charles's heart. Travis helped himself to bacon and eggs, sat down and began eating. The legal complications of purchasing the island, and the logistical complications of erecting a castle on it, happily occupied Charles for the next half hour. Then he pushed back his chair. "Finished, Travis?" he asked. "Why don't we go to the library? Julie, I'll meet you at the courts in about an hour. The rackets are kept in the club house."

"I'll look forward to it," Julie said.

After refilling his coffee cup, Travis followed Charles to the library. His father closed the door, then took up a position in front of the hearth. He looked extremely ill at ease. Was he about to discuss changes in his will, changes that possibly disinherited his elder son? Financially Travis couldn't care less; emotionally he cared quite a lot.

He leaned against a leather wing chair. Nothing in the

library had changed. The same prints on the walls, the same array of leatherbound and doubtless unread classics. He himself had discovered Kipling here, C.S. Lewis and Tolkien, all the heroes who had peopled his childhood. He said casually, "What's on your mind, Dad?"

Charles said pompously, "You must understand that your arrival last night was a shock to us all."

"I hope the shock wasn't too unpleasant."

"I possibly said things I shouldn't have, on the patio after dinner," Charles labored on. "I apologize for that."

It was more than Travis had expected. He said warmly, more than willing to meet his father half way, "You're forgiven."

Staring fixedly at the door behind his son's back, Charles said, "A reconciliation is, of course, what we all want. You're right, the past is the past and should be forgotten. Bygones be bygones. The hatchet buried."

Charles had always favored clichés. "I'm very willing to do that," Travis said, trying to disguise the fact that he was inwardly puzzled. This was all too easy. Had Charles really had such a huge change of heart overnight?

"That disgraceful media attack, the ring…water under the bridge."

"I've often regretted that I went to the papers. It was the action of an adolescent, that's all I can say. I wouldn't handle it that way now."

"Yes, yes," Charles said impatiently.

But Travis hadn't finished. His voice rough with the intensity of his feelings, he said, "As for the ring, I swear I didn't take it."

"Never mind the ring, I don't really miss it anymore. So everything's forgiven and forgotten and now you can leave Portland right away. No reason to hang around. You've done what you set out to do."

Looking rather pleased with himself, Charles bounced up

and down on the soles of his handmade Italian loafers. "Leave Portland?" Travis repeated.

"Well yes. Of course. Why would you stay in a little backwater town like Portland?" Charles said bluffly. "I'm sure you've got bigger fish to fry. I've read about you over the years, some of your successes in establishing new hospitals and revitalizing old ones in all those third world countries. Very important work, Travis. Vital. I'm sure you're anxious to get back to it. I can understand you might have thought it would take all summer to soften my attitude, and that's why you allowed two months." He gave a hearty laugh. "I've taken you by surprise, haven't I? You thought I'd be much more adamant."

"I did, yes." Thinking furiously, Travis said, "I'm very glad we're having this conversation, and I look forward to many more. But I can't leave Portland right away—I made a commitment to Mark and his family."

"You can't leave? Of course you can."

Julie was also living in Portland, at least temporarily. Julie and he had some unfinished business. Travis said easily, "I'll be gone by the first of September."

"Get someone else to fill in for your friend!"

"What's the rush, Dad? If you've really forgiven me, why wouldn't you want to spend some time with me?"

"Your stepmother and I are going to be exceptionally busy this summer. We may even go away for a month or more…perhaps you could come to Boston for Christmas."

"Perhaps I could." Although he'd long hated the luxurious mansion in Back Bay. "Let's play it by ear…there's been a big gap in our relationship, and we can't patch it up overnight."

"So you'll leave Portland?" Charles said eagerly.

"I've explained why I can't do that right away."

Charles pursed his lips. "I'm asking a favor of you, Travis. Surely after all these years, you can do one small thing for me. Find a substitute—there must be lots of doctors who'd be happy to spend the rest of the summer in Maine.''

"If I understood why you want me to leave, I might be more open to doing so.''

With vicious emphasis, Charles said, "Why was your favorite word as a little boy. You could never accept anything at face value, you always had to be poking and prying for reasons. You haven't changed, Travis, you're just the same as you always were.''

So the forgiveness was only skin deep. Travis said carefully, "I'll be talking to Mark next week, I'll see what he says. It's the best I can do.''

"It's little enough," Charles huffed. "And now I must go and change if I'm to meet Julie." He gave his son a sharp nod. "Take my advice—call Mark as soon as possible.''

He marched past Travis and shut the door behind him with unnecessary force. Travis gazed after him unseeingly. What was going on? And what was he missing? Had that been Charles's inept attempt at a genuine reconciliation? Or had it been fake from the start?

But why?

Which was indeed one of his favorite words, he thought wryly. Why would Charles want him to leave Portland tomorrow?

And why was Julie the main reason he didn't want to?

CHAPTER SIX

AT SEVEN-THIRTY that evening, Travis straightened his tie in the bathroom mirror, adjusted his tuxedo jacket and knew he couldn't delay going downstairs any longer. He'd faced guerillas, epidemics, droughts and floods the last few years. And now he was scared of a crowd of his father's friends?

Put it any way you like, he wasn't looking forward to the evening. Too many people, too many of whom would be less than delighted to see him, coupled with the necessity to behave as though there really had been a reconciliation between himself and his father.

If he'd wanted to be an actor, he wouldn't have gone to medical school.

Not for the first time, he wished his sister Jenessa was here as well. Although he hadn't seen a lot of her since he'd turned sixteen, he'd made a point of staying in touch with her. Beautiful, wayward and artistic, Jenessa was gradually making a name for herself among the galleries and collectors that mattered; Travis had always admired her fierce determination to go her own way. Right now, he could have done with her moral support.

Resolutely Travis left his room and ran down the curved staircase. All afternoon the guests had been arriving in their yachts, cabin cruisers and private seaplanes. Now the party eddied among the tents set up on the lawn, each lit by tiny white lights that glimmered like fireflies. There were enough potted plants to stock every flower shop in New York, and enough jewels on the women to buy the White House. He made his way to the main tent, stopping to talk

52

to people on the way, ironically amused to note those of his father's friends who turned their backs before he could speak to them.

Bankers and stockbrokers tended to have long memories: they wouldn't have forgotten or forgiven that long-ago newspaper article. He sighted Brent at the bar with a blond in a dress that highlighted at least two of her obvious assets, and looked around for Julie. His gaze sharpened as he saw her among a crowd of younger guests at the far end of the lawn, as far from Brent as she could get. She hadn't seen him. He moved closer, his heart thudding over the sound of the band.

Her dress was of raw Thai silk, slit to the knee, its simple lines and thin straps elegant rather than overtly provocative, its subtle blending of blues and greens emphasizing her eyes. A delicate gauze scarf floated from the neckline, her shoulders gleaming through its soft folds. Brazilian crystal shimmered around her throat and at her lobes.

He had to have her. He had to.

But not here. Not now. Later.

The words had come unbidden. But every nerve in Travis's body told him they were true. He'd never in his life desired a woman so imperatively, with such fierce impatience.

He turned away, going back to the main tent, where he joined Charles and Corinne for a celebratory glass of champagne, danced with Corinne and a couple of her friends, and ate supper with the old family doctor and his wife, long allies of his. It was dark by the time he went in search of Julie.

She was dancing to some raucous rock and roll in the tent closest to the water. Slim and lissome, her hips moving with a sensuality that caught at his throat, she looked as though she was having a wonderful time. Her partner was a tall, bearded young man. Not for long, Travis thought, waiting until the song ended before heading for the dance floor. He came up behind her and looped an arm around her waist. "Hello, Julie."

A tremor ran through her body; she froze in the circle of his arm. Then she turned as awkwardly as a puppet. "Travis," she mumbled. With an obvious effort she added, "Do you know these people?"

The tall young man's name was Michael, and his plump pretty wife was called Kathy. "The next dance is mine," Travis said.

The music had started again. Under cover of the bass Julie hissed, "Are you asking me or telling me?"

She hadn't meant her ill temper to show. But all evening she'd been waiting for him to find her, catching occasional glimpses of him, furious that he should so cavalierly ignore her. Travis said abruptly, "You're right, we don't need to dance. Do you want something to eat?"

"I've already eaten."

"Let's go for a walk down by the water."

"You ignore me all evening and now I'm supposed to jump ten feet high the minute you say so? I don't think so."

"Julie," he said, "I've danced with Corinne, I made a speech that was a miracle of diplomacy when they toasted my father, I've been snubbed by two-thirds of his friends, and I need ten minutes away from it all." He'd also been publicly hugged by Charles, briefly, but nonetheless an embrace. One Brent had witnessed, he thought with a quiver of unease.

Julie looked up at him more closely. There were lines of strain bracketing his mouth and his eyes looked dark and depthless. Suddenly she was tired of deception. "Last night I was on my balcony when you and your family came out on the patio. I overheard everything that was said, from the death of your mother to the disappearance of the family ring.''

Travis looked down at her, his jawline hard with tension. He'd always guarded his privacy: a strategy that had served him well over the years. He didn't like Julie knowing all the Strathern secrets; other than Bryce, no one knew about his past. ''Do you make a habit of listening to other people's conversations?'' he rasped.

She tilted her chin. ''Sure…it's how I get my kicks.''

Travis disliked subservient women; he didn't have a worry in the world about Julie. ''My father, for some unknown reason, wants me to leave Portland within the week.''

''Are you going to?''

''No,'' Travis said. ''I'm not much good at doing what I'm told. I'll stay until the end of the summer.''

Julie looked at him in silence. Portland was a small city. Too small for both of them; she herself had signed a three-month contract. She said, ''I can't go for a walk with you right now. I promised Kathy and Michael I'd go with them when she feeds the baby…I went to school with her and Michael, and she's dying to show off her daughter. Oh, she's waving at me now.''

''I'll come with you,'' Travis said.

''I don't think—''

''Hey, Julie,'' Kathy said. ''The sitter just called on the cell phone, Andrea's awake. Travis, do you want to see our new addition? Three months old tomorrow.''

''Sure,'' he said easily, and tucked Julie's hand in his arm. ''Let's go.''

Julie's feet were killing her in her new silver sandals, and she felt thoroughly out of sorts. She also felt as lustful as a stray cat under a full moon. She walked across the grass toward the castle, trying to keep as far from Travis as she could, every fiber in her body aware of his long, easy stride. If only he wasn't so tall, so male, so damnably handsome. When she added to that a velvet-soft evening filled with the scent of roses and the tumble of waves on the beach, she was done for.

The baby was in a crib in a bedroom on the ground floor, where a lamp threw golden light over the furniture. Kathy picked her daughter up, while Michael went with the sitter to the nearby kitchen to heat a bottle. "Here, Julie, hold Andrea for a minute," Kathy said. "I've got to dig out a clean diaper."

The baby was thrust into Julie's arms. Instinctively she cupped the little head with its dark fuzz of hair to her shoulder, supporting the baby's spine with her other hand. The warmth of the small body, and Andrea's fretful whimpering filled her with a deep tenderness.

Travis had stationed himself by the door, his eyes glued to the woman holding the baby, his heart beating like a triphammer. If he'd had a camera, he'd have taken a photo of her: Woman with Child. But why did he need a camera? Wasn't her image engraved on his mind?

How little he really knew about her! About her dreams and desires, the betrayals of her past and her needs. He'd always thought of himself as reasonably astute. But she was an enigma.

As though the intensity of Travis's gaze was a pull she couldn't gainsay, Julie glanced up. His eyes seemed to see right into her soul. She held Andrea a little more tightly, trying desperately to look anywhere but at him. And failed.

"Put her down on the bed, Julie," Kathy said. "What's up? Are you okay?"

"Oh…yes, I'm fine," Julie stumbled, and laid the baby on the flannel blanket. Her arms felt empty, her body cold. Warm me, Travis, she thought, warm me.

Knowing she had no choice, she crossed the room toward him. As he put an arm around her shoulders, she leaned into his body, into its solidity and heat, closing her eyes. She couldn't cry. Not here. Not now.

Why would she want to cry? Travis was a stranger, chance-met, soon to be gone from her life.

Travis said softly, "Hold still, the baby dribbled on your shoulder." Gently he started scrubbing at her gauze scarf where it rested on her bare skin, using a tissue he'd taken from his pocket.

Why couldn't she have him? What was to stop her?

The thought had dropped into her mind without any warning. Calling on every ounce of her resolve, Julie straightened, pulling away from him. "Thanks," she said briefly. "Kathy, we'll leave you to it. I'm so glad we met this evening, let's get together in the next couple of weeks."

"Our number's in the book. Give us a call." Kathy chuckled. "Just not too early in the morning."

"She's a lovely baby," Julie said sincerely. "Ready, Travis?"

She walked out of the room ahead of him, her spine very straight. She had no idea how to find her room from here. But find it she had to. And alone.

As they walked back out into the garden, Travis said, "So what was that all about?"

"What do you mean?"

"You almost ran into my arms. Then you backed off as if I were the devil himself."

"You see too much," she said in an unfriendly voice. "I'm tired, and I've had more than enough of this party— I'm going to my room. I'll see you tomorrow."

They were standing in the shadows of the lilac bushes that, long ago, his mother had adored for their scent. One of his earliest memories was of her carrying an armload of purple blooms into the living room and arranging them in a deep copper bowl. Her long black hair had been pinned to her head in lustrous waves; as a little boy he'd likened them to the black sheen of the sea on a winter's evening.

With an effort Travis wrenched himself back to the present. He'd lost his mother. But he was damned if he was going to let Julie walk away from him as if he were nothing but a stick of furniture.

He put his arms around her, pulling her into his body, and lowered his head to her shoulder, smoothing it with his mouth. Her skin was delicately scented; her response quivered through her. He traced the rise of her shoulder to her neck, then dropped to find the pulse at the base of her throat: a pulse racing like that of a bird. And all the while his hands were molding the long curve of her spine all the way to the flare of her hips, learning her, memorizing her. Desire engulfed him, fierce and imperative.

He raised his head to kiss her, unerringly finding her lips in the dark, teasing them open and plunging with his tongue. She was trembling very lightly in his embrace. Slow down, he thought, and with all his willpower gentled his kiss, searching out the sweetness of her mouth.

She arched against him with a moan of surrender that filled Travis with exultation. Her hands were under his jacket, roaming the flat plane of his chest, fitting themselves to his rib cage, then pulling him closer until he was unutterably frustrated by the layers of clothing between his flesh and hers. "Julie," he muttered against her mouth, "let's go to my room. I want you in my bed."

She heard him from a long way away, through a haze of passion as vivid as sunset, as compelling as the tides of the sea. Compelling. Irresistible. She herself out of control in a way that was foreign to her.

Out of control.

She reared back, panic-stricken. She'd never felt this way with a man before; she'd always been able to call the shots. If she made love with Travis, all that would change. He'd have power over her. She knew it in her bones. Power over her forever.

Joke, Julie. Make a joke of it. She said breathlessly, "Are you the college chemistry course that I missed? Your body plus my body, a good dose of lilacs as the catalyst, and an explosion's guaranteed?"

Travis cupped her face in his palms, his forefingers molding her cheekbones. "You can skip the lilacs."

"Lilacs or not, I'm out of here, Travis," she gasped. "You're too much for me."

"Scared, Julie?"

"Chemistry never was my strong point."

He said softly, running his hands over the silken darkness of her hair, "Did you like biology better?"

She managed a credible laugh, forcing herself to step backward from the heat of his body. "Physics was my forte," she said, and abandoned any attempt at humor. "Travis, I'm not looking for an affair. Whether it's just this weekend, or the rest of the summer, it's not in my plans."

"Didn't your chemistry professor ever tell you about spontaneous combustion?"

"I must have missed that lecture."

"We don't need a lecture. Just you and me under the stars."

She was suddenly exhausted. She couldn't take anymore. "I don't want to do something we'd both regret," she said sharply.

"Don't speak for me, Julie...I wouldn't regret it. Some guy must have hurt you really badly, am I right?"

If only it were that simple. But if that's what he wanted to think, let him. "Good night," she said, "I'll see you tomorrow." Then she picked up her skirts and ran away from him across the grass.

Travis watched her go. He could easily have caught up with her, and certainly he could have physically overpowered her. But was that what he wanted? Or did he want Julie to walk into his arms of her own volition? Clear-eyed and willing.

He had at the most two months in which to achieve that aim. But he'd never backed down from a challenge in his life, and he wasn't going to start now. Not when the prize was a woman whose body called to his in the most powerful way possible.

He had to possess her. And he would.

CHAPTER SEVEN

THE woods were lush and green, her feet sinking into a thick carpet of sphagnum moss, ferns brushing her bare knees. As Julie stood still, relishing the silence and peace, a bright yellow warbler landed on a branch just above her, looking at her with its dark eye.

Once again, she'd slept badly. And once again, she'd dreamed about Travis. Unrepeatable dreams. X-rated. No one under the age of eighteen admitted.

But at least she'd had the sense to run away from him last night in the shadow of the lilacs.

Julie sighed. Hadn't her expedition this morning also been related to Travis? Another attempt to put distance between him and her? She was on the island offshore to Manatuck, the kayak she'd borrowed from the boathouse pulled up on the shale beach. As far as she could tell, this island was completely unspoiled. No one living on it, and certainly no stone castles. It had a serenity Manatuck lacked; idly she found herself wondering who was lucky enough to own it.

With a quiver of unease she wondered if her wandering lifestyle was starting to pall. Certainly she missed the rocky shores and crisp blue waves of home more and more with each departure.

Settle in Portland? No way.

She'd explore for a few minutes, then head back to Castlereigh in lots of time for breakfast. Quite a few of the guests had stayed overnight; breakfast would be a very sociable affair. Again, all the better to hide from Travis. And then she'd leave Manatuck on the launch, and go back to her daily life.

She wished Travis was leaving Portland this week, as his father wanted him to.

Her illusory peace shattered, Julie wandered back down the slope, picking her footholds with care, because the rocks among the moss were wet with dew. As she emerged from the trees, she saw with an unpleasant tightening of her nerves that a second kayak had been pulled up on the beach. Brent was striding up the shale toward the trees.

Brent. Not Travis.

"Good morning," she called. "You're up early."

He didn't bother answering, too intent on closing the distance between them. She stationed herself beside a fallen log, feeling her heartbeat quicken. There wasn't another soul on this island other than herself and Brent. She didn't like Brent, nor did she trust him.

He stopped two feet away from her. "This island belongs to Travis," he said. "Did you know that?"

"No."

"Yeah...our grandfather left it to him. Along with a big bundle of money."

She stated the obvious. "You hate your brother."

"Did you see him and Dad last night? A touching little display of filial love. Of course Travis wants a reconciliation, he knows which side his bread's buttered on."

Julie might be terrified of making love with Travis; but she wasn't blind to his character, and somehow she doubted that he was driven by mercenary motives. "You're judging him by your own standards," she said with more truth than wisdom.

"Clever little Julie...you dropped me as soon as you saw him, didn't you?"

"I dropped you when you forced your way into my room."

"You should have thought twice before coming out to this island all by yourself."

"Come off it, Brent," she said sharply. "Strong-arm stuff is punishable by law, or hadn't you noticed? And just to keep the record straight, I'm no more interested in having an affair with Travis than I am with you. I told him so last night."

"You expect me to believe that? I wasn't born yesterday."

"If you weren't born yesterday, then use your common sense and go back to Manatuck. I'll be along in time for breakfast."

"I don't think so," he said.

As his eyes narrowed and his muscles tensed, Julie had a split-second to react. Pivoting, she raced for the shelter of the woods. Brent wasn't in good shape like Travis; she was almost certain she could outrun him. She could hear him close behind her, too close, swearing in a steady monotone that raised the hairs on the back of her neck. She leaped a fallen trunk, slipped on a rock, regained her balance and dashed between two trees. A snag tore at her arm; all she could hear was the drumming of her heart in her ears, and Brent's harsh breathing.

Still too close. And she dared not look back.

Fear lending her wings, she took what looked like a pathway through the trees straight up the slope, still trusting that she could outlast him. Inwardly giving thanks that she'd attended her fitness club so faithfully, she ran hard for several minutes. Then, her lungs heaving for air, she dodged some shrubs, ducked under a couple of low branches and scrambled up a sheer face of granite with an agility that, even in the moment, amused her. She couldn't have done it in cold blood; she'd never liked heights. Darting through some pines, their soft needles giving her a better foothold, she ran on.

She didn't even see the hollow in the ground, burrow of some unknown animal. One foot went down the hole, throwing her off balance. By flinging herself sideways, Julie managed to avoid twisting her ankle. But she landed hard, a broken branch ripping at her leg. With a gasp of pain, she struggled to her feet and staggered on.

But there was no heavy breathing behind her. Had she, despite her fall, outrun Brent?

She threw a glance over her shoulder. Boughs gently waving in the breeze, ferns and rusted needles on the forest floor, and no sign of her pursuer. She was alone in the woods. More slowly, she went further into the pines, then changed direction to throw Brent off in case he was still following her. When she was certain she really was alone, Julie sank down on a granite boulder, her eyes still darting this way and that.

Her leg was bleeding very messily, she'd scraped her palm when she landed, and her cheekbone was bruised and sore. But at least, she thought, cheering up, she hadn't twisted or broken her ankle. All she had to do was wait for a while, then creep back down to the shore. If there was only one kayak left on the beach, then Brent was gone.

Taking her time, limping slightly, Julie put this plan into action twenty minutes later. But when she finally emerged from the trees, she saw to her dismay that both kayaks were gone.

Wrong beach. It must be.

It wasn't. She recognized the reef that she'd rounded to approach the beach. Brent had towed her kayak away.

She said every swearword that she knew, in every language she'd ever been exposed to. While this made her feel better, it didn't produce a second kayak. The tide had turned, the current streaming past the rocks. She couldn't swim back to Manatuck, she'd be swept out to sea.

Great, she thought. Just great. Now what should she do?

Her mad dash through the trees had made her thirsty and given her an appetite; but her water bottle and trail mix were tucked down beside the seat of her kayak. Her only option was to swim back once the tidal rip subsided. In three or four hours, she thought glumly.

How long before she was missed? Would Travis notice she was gone? Or would he assume she'd already left on the launch without saying goodbye? Which, after the way she'd run away from him last night, he'd be entirely justified in doing.

Maybe he'd already left Manatuck himself.

One thing was sure. Brent wouldn't tell anyone where she was.

Travis, unusually for him, slept late that morning, so it was well past nine when he went down for breakfast. He hesitated outside Julie's bedroom door, tapped on the panels, and knew intuitively from the silence that the room was empty. So she must be downstairs.

He ran down to the dining room, crowded with those guests who had spent the night rather than be ferried out to their yachts at two in the morning. Tables and chairs had been set out on the patio, overflowing onto the lawn. Julie was nowhere to be seen. He cornered Charles by the coffeepot. "Have you seen Julie?"

"No, come to think of it, I haven't." Charles chuckled. "I showed her a new spin on her serve, maybe she's practising."

Corinne hadn't seen her, either. She said coolly, "Brent left for the mainland an hour ago with Oliver. Maybe she went with him."

His gut lurched. "Did she say goodbye to you?"

"No. But there's been such a crush of people…oh, there are the Hallidays, I must speak to them. Excuse me, Travis."

Travis stared after her, fighting down a confusion of emotion. Would Julie have left with Brent, without saying goodbye to her host and hostess? He didn't think so; but then, what did he really know about her?

The key question was whether she'd left with Brent. She'd promised to stay away from him; but was she trustworthy?

If she hadn't left with Brent, where was she?

He checked the tennis courts and the pool, without any luck. Then he hurried down to the boathouse. Alongside a small powerboat, four kayaks were moored. A pair of dark glasses was tucked under the bungee cords of the red one. Julie's glasses. She'd been wearing them yesterday afternoon.

A water bottle and a bag of nuts and raisins lay on the seat. His head swiveled around as the door creaked open. But it was one of the groundsmen, not Julie. He said urgently, "Did anyone go kayaking this morning, Russell?"

"I saw Mr. Brent about an hour ago, towing a second kayak from Bear Island. I thought it was kinda funny at the time."

"Towing it—empty?"

"Yep. Just him. Then he took off in the launch with Oliver."

"By himself?"

Russell kept his face expressionless. "Him and a blond lady, sir."

That would be the blonde who'd been wrapped around Brent most of last night. So Julie hadn't left with Brent. "Thanks, Russell," Travis said and knew exactly what he was going to do.

Twenty minutes later, Travis was paddling around the northeast shoals of Manatuck, Bear Island now in sight. Brent was smart enough to know that he couldn't get away with violence. He wouldn't have hurt Julie and left her on the island. Would he?

If he had, there'd be hell to pay, Travis thought grimly. There was a cold lump of dread lodged in his gut; it was taking a huge effort to prevent that dread from turning into outright terror. What had Brent done to Julie? Why had he towed an empty kayak back to Manatuck? Julie was no pushover, she wouldn't have sat by meekly and allowed his brother to leave her stranded on an uninhabited island.

He'd gone far enough north for the tide to carry him toward the beach on the island that he owned. Steering with all his strength, because he was alone in a double kayak, he passed the reefs and saw the long stretch of shale in front of him. Using rudder and paddle, he headed straight for it, jamming the prow of the kayak up onto the rocks. Swiftly he climbed out and hauled his craft out of reach of the tide.

Then he looked up. A woman was walking from the shade of the trees onto the sun-drenched shale. She was limping.

His first reaction was a relief so overpowering that he felt almost dizzy. Julie was safe. Alive and well. It wasn't until now that he could admit to himself how terrified he'd been of the alternative, despite his inner conviction that Brent was too self-serving to do real harm.

His second reaction, predictably, was anger. He strode across the beach toward her, his soft-soled sneakers crunching the shale. "Are you okay?" he rapped.

Julie nodded. "I'm glad to see you," she said with a small smile.

He didn't smile back. "Did Brent leave you here?"

"Yes."

"If he laid as much as a finger on you, I'll have his hide for a floor mat."

"He didn't. I ran away," she said economically.

"Your leg's bleeding."

"I tripped and fell. Can we go back, Travis? I'm hungry, thirsty, and in dire need of a shower."

"We'll go back in a minute," he said, each word dropping like a stone. "Will you kindly explain to me what you and Brent were doing out here in the first place? You promised to stay away from him."

Her chin snapped up. "Are you insinuating I came out here with him?"

"The thought had occurred to me, yes."

"And why would I have done that?"

"You tell me."

"I came out here by myself to get some peace and quiet before breakfast. Brent must have seen me and followed me. Although why I'm bothering to explain this to you when you persist in thinking the worst of me, I have no idea. Take me back to Manatuck, Travis—now. And spare me the sermons, I don't need them."

"If you'd stayed away from Brent in the first place, you wouldn't be in this mess," Travis said furiously.

"And I wouldn't have met you. Which certainly would be a bonus."

"Your cheek—did he hit you?"

"I told you—he didn't as much as touch me!"

"Dammit, Julie, ever since I saw your dark glasses on the kayak in the boathouse, I've been picturing you drowned, raped and murdered," Travis said in a voice raw with emotion.

Too much emotion, he thought distantly. Far too much. But it was too late to take it back.

She let out her breath in a long sigh. "I'm hungry, thirsty and sore. Not drowned, raped or murdered. So why are we standing here yelling at each other?"

"Because I was worried sick about you."

"I get the message." She scowled at him. "I bet all the bacon and eggs will be gone by the time we get back."

"I'll have Bertram order you a breakfast all of your own. He owes you, after leaving the room keys hanging in the pantry."

Looking somewhat more cheerful, Julie said, "You'd do that for me?"

"I'd do a lot more than that for you," Travis said harshly; and listened to the words echo in his head.

"Bacon and eggs would be plenty, thank you."

"Are you warning me off?"

"I don't know!"

Travis took a step back. "Let's go."

"I've hurt you, haven't I?" she whispered. "I'm sorry, Travis, I—"

"Your imagination's working overtime."

"So you don't hurt, like ordinary people?" she lashed.

"I quit that a long time ago."

"I don't believe you!"

"That's your choice," he said curtly. "In the meantime, we can argue half the morning, or we can paddle back to Manatuck."

"Arguing with you is a lost cause," Julie snapped, and turned away, marching down the shore toward the kayak.

Travis stayed where he was. He hated how easily she could get to him. On top of that, he wanted to kiss her so badly he could taste the sweetness of her lips against his. He didn't want to think what he might have done had Brent harmed her. He was a doctor, for God's sake. He was supposed to heal, not hurt.

Raking his fingers through his hair, his footsteps crunching on the barnacles, Travis followed Julie down to the kayak. Once there, he passed her the water bottle and trail mix, watching the movements of her throat as she swallowed. Added to the terror and rage he'd felt earlier was another, disturbingly new emotion: a fierce instinct to protect her from further harm.

Coupled with, of course, the ever-present gnawing of desire. Not that yelling at her on a lonely beach was the way to entice her into his bed. He had to come up with a better strategy than that.

Julie took a handful of nuts from the bag. "Nothing like a few raisins and almonds for making life worth living. Want some?"

Desire wasn't on her mind. For sure.

Travis chewed a few peanuts that might as well have been wood chips and said abruptly, "We'd better get going. We'll follow the beach and the reefs north, then cut across the channel above Manatuck."

Which is what they did. Julie was an adept and strong kayaker, their paddles flashing in unison; Travis knew better than to see this as a metaphor.

They docked in the boathouse, then Travis led the way through the trees to a side door where they'd be unlikely to meet any of his father's guests. The back stairs took them to the far end of the wing where their bedrooms were located. Outside her door he said, "I'll wait for you while you shower. Then I want to check that gash in your leg, you don't want to risk infection."

"I can look after it."

"Julie, I'm a doctor," he said coldly. "This isn't a come-on."

She flushed. "You've got a practice in Portland?"

"Just for the summer. Filling in for Mark MacDonald."

"I'm a physiotherapist," she said rapidly. "So I know enough first aid to look after myself."

This was new information to Travis. Ever since he'd met Julie, he'd been so off balance he'd never thought to ask the ordinary questions, like her age or what she did to earn her living. "Do you work in the hospital? Why haven't I seen you there?"

If she answered him, Julie thought, he'd know where to find her. With huge reluctance she said, "I've got a temporary contract at Silversides, the clinic just out of town."

She knew as well as he that Silversides was a retreat for the very rich; just as she knew Dr. MacDonald's practice was almost exclusively white-collar. She could have told him about her real work overseas; but why bother? After today, she wasn't going to see him again.

"I'll get my bag," he said. "I always travel with it."

"You're like a nor'easter," she said irritably, "there's no stopping you."

"And you don't have to worry about Brent, he left on the launch. With a blonde."

"It isn't Brent I'm worrying about," Julie said unwisely and shut the door in Travis's face.

The hot water stung her various cuts and scrapes; she was going to have a few choice bruises when she went back to work tomorrow. She pulled on her sundress, brushed her hair and left the bathroom.

Travis was sitting on the bed, looking very much at home. He'd changed into cotton trousers and a blue shirt open at the neck, the sleeves rolled up. Suppressing the urge to jump him, Julie said, "Make it fast, I'm hungry."

Recklessly she plunked herself down beside him on the bed, hauling her skirt above her knees. She wasn't going to jump him. She knew better than to do that.

So she was quite safe.

CHAPTER EIGHT

THE scrape on Julie's knee was picturesque and hurt like crazy; but it wasn't overly deep. Travis knelt in front of her, extracting a few specks of bark with sterile tweezers, then smoothing on antibiotic ointment and applying a light bandage. Julie watched him, fascinated by the skill of his long fingers, so deft and gentle. He'd be a very good doctor.

He'd be a very good lover.

Desire washed over her, so strongly that it was as much as she could do to keep her hands at her sides. "Keep an eye on it," Travis said, getting to his feet.

Her face must have been an open book. With a strangled sound in his throat, Travis pushed her back on the bed, threw himself down beside her and began kissing her, fiercely possessive kisses that sang along her veins until the beat of her blood was like a primitive drum. She kissed him back, running her hands through the thick silkiness of his hair, stroking his nape, roaming his muscled shoulders. As he tugged at the hem of his shirt, she went lower, desperate to feel skin and flesh. The rough hair on his belly tangled her fingers; and then she found his nipple, hard as a pebble.

His tongue twined with hers in an intimacy that served only to increase her hunger. She opened to him, whimpering with need; and felt him slide the straps from her shoulders, pulling her dress down to bare her breasts. As he cupped them in his palms, she arched toward him, aching for more, maddened by sensations that were building as inexorably as a storm at sea.

His head dropped to her breast, his mouth taking one tip

then the other, laving them until she was moaning with pleasure. When he raised his head to kiss her mouth again, she tore at the buttons on his shirt; then she pulled him down to lie on her, the roughness of his body hair abrading her breasts.

Her skirt was above her thighs. At the first touch of his fingers between her legs, she gave a strangled cry. All the barriers were down; as the hardness of his erection dug into her thigh, she knew she couldn't rest until he was inside her. Where he belonged.

But even as she fumbled to remove the scrap of lace that was keeping him from her, Travis reared up, his eyes fastened on her face. "Julie," he said hoarsely, "in a moment I won't be able to stop. Is this what you want?"

She looked at him blankly, trying to find her voice. "Of course it is," she gasped, "can't you tell?"

"A summer affair."

It was as though he were trying the words out, she thought, listening to see how they sounded. Only last night she'd told him an affair was the last thing she was looking for; and she'd meant it. But now, crazed by passion, she was just about begging him to take her.

In a cracked voice she said, "I want you so much that I forgot all the reasons we shouldn't be doing this."

Pushing him off, she sat up; as she dragged at her dress to hide her breasts, the words came tumbling from her lips. "I thought I knew myself until you came along. I'm no virgin, Travis—when I was twenty I went to bed with my physics partner, because I figured it was time I found out what sex was all about. Nothing much, that's what I discovered. No big deal. So I got on with my life. And that was fine with me, I didn't want to fall in love back then and I still don't. And I sure don't want to get married."

She paused for breath, her hands clasped in her lap. "I've dated since then, of course I have. Nice men, attractive men, many of whom would have been happy to have an affair with no strings attached. But I never did. Not one of them swept me off my feet. Until you came along.'' She bit her lip. ''I don't understand why you're so different. When you kiss me, I forget everything except you. You saw how I behaved a moment ago, I was like a wild woman. That's not me! I've never been like that.''

''You think I come on to women I've only just met?''

''How would I know?''

He said with vicious truth, ''Whatever's swept you off your feet has knocked the feet right out from under me.''

''And how you hate me for doing that to you!''

''Why don't you want to fall in love or get married?''

He'd gone right to the crux. ''Two reasons,'' she said with an unhappy laugh. ''My father and my mother. And that's all you're getting out of me.'' In a flurry of skirts, she stood up. ''I'm sorry if I seemed to be leading you on, I couldn't help myself. I'm going downstairs for breakfast and then I'll leave with Oliver.''

''I was a damn fool to ask if you really wanted to make love,'' Travis said harshly. ''If we'd just gone ahead and done it, you wouldn't be in such a rush to get on the boat.''

Her knee was hurting, her whole body was a huge ache of sexual frustration, and all she wanted to do was curl up on the bed and sob her heart out. ''I'm glad you did ask. It's better for both of us this way.''

He pushed himself to his feet. ''We'll be in Portland for the summer, you and I. We're bound to meet up with each other.''

''I'll do my best to see that doesn't happen.''

''So this is goodbye,'' he said in an unreadable voice.

She gave him the faintest of smiles. ''You'll have forgotten me in a couple of days, you'll see.''

''Don't judge me by your own standards!''

Flinching from the fury in his face, Julie shoved her feet

into her sandals and ran for the door. But his voice stopped her, pinioning her to the white-painted panels. "You're planning on forgetting me. On forgetting what happens every time we get within ten feet of each other. Aren't you?"

"I've got to!"

"Maybe it's time you started behaving like an adult instead of jerking me around like a puppet on a string. On one minute, off the next. Or are you going to let your parents run your life for the rest of your days?"

"You didn't have to kiss me, Travis."

"You know what I really hate? That I didn't have a choice," he said savagely.

"We all have choices," she retorted. "And I'm choosing to get out of here before we do any more damage."

"I wouldn't have called you a coward," he jeered. "Goodbye, Julie...have a nice life."

She made a sound expressive of fury and frustration, whirled and banged the door shut behind her. Impossible man. Infuriating, arrogant and irresistibly sexy man. Scowling prodigiously, wincing at the pain in her knee, Julie went downstairs and hurried across the hall. She stopped short at the dining-room door, pasted a smile on her face and pushed it open. The huge table was spread with ample bacon and eggs, along with a gorgeous array of fruit, freshly baked croissants and coffee cakes. She stood still in the doorway; her appetite had completely forsaken her.

Forcing herself to calm down, she went in search of Charles and Corinne. They were outside on the patio. Calling on all her good manners, she thanked them for a wonderful stay and made her escape. When she went back to her room to get her bag, there was no sign of Travis. Nor was he, to her infinite relief, on the dock by the boathouse. Oliver was leaving in five minutes, he told her. She waited in an agony of impatience, making conversation with four other guests who were also leaving Manatuck. They all climbed aboard, and the launch pulled away from the dock.

She went to stand by the bow. As the island receded, she stole one last glance at it. But it wasn't the crenellated towers and absurd turrets, or the bannered tents on the lawn that held her attention. It was the lighthouse at the northeast tip of the island, where a dark-haired man had kissed her on the grass, turning her into a woman she didn't even recognize.

A woman of passion, who was afraid of that passion. More afraid than she'd ever been of anything in her life.

Left alone in Julie's bedroom, Travis stared unseeingly out of the window. He'd made a fool of himself. A total and unmitigated fool. Telling her she'd knocked him off his feet. Rambling on about having no choice.

He'd been on the brink of begging her to go to bed with him. Begging? Him?

Thank heavens he hadn't sunk that low.

But how was he ever going to forget the sweet rise of her breast, the racing of her pulse against his palm, the delicate scent of her skin? Or the brilliant green of her irises when he'd kissed her, their depths shot with fire? Why in hell had he blabbed on about summer affairs, giving her the time to think?

If he hadn't, she'd have been his.

He banged his fist hard on the sill, almost relishing the pain. If he'd been all kinds of a fool, at least he wasn't going to repeat his mistakes. He'd make sure of that by never seeing her again. He only rarely went to the clinic, and by the sound of it she wouldn't come near the hospital; plus he had no intention of finding out her phone number.

What did he need her phone number for when he wasn't going to see her again?

Goodbye meant just that. Goodbye.

He was well rid of Julie Renshaw.

Travis stayed on Manatuck until the last of the guests had gone. He, Corinne and Charles ate an informal supper on the patio, Travis doing his best to sound more at ease than he felt. Then he got up. "I'll get my bag, I told Oliver I'd be leaving in a few minutes."

"Fine, fine," Charles said. "Glad you could make it for the party, Travis. You remember what I said...Portland's too small for you, you'd be better off heading overseas where there's more scope for your talents."

"I hear you, Dad." One more person who didn't want to see him again, he thought with an inward wince. "Goodbye, Corinne," he added, "thanks for everything."

She offered him the same cool cheek as when he'd arrived, just as though the intervening two days hadn't happened. It was left for Oliver to say at the wharf on the mainland, "You come back soon, Mr. Travis. Manatuck ain't the same without you."

"Thanks, Oliver. Take care."

Julie's blue car was, of course, gone. Travis drove back to Portland, parking his car and going upstairs to the condo that belonged to Mark MacDonald and that he was renting for the summer. It was a very desirable condo built on one of the wharves on the waterfront, in sight of yachts and ferries and lobster boats. He'd made very little attempt to imprint his personality on it; as he entered, its impersonality struck him like a blow.

He wanted Julie here with him. That's what he wanted.

Dammit, he didn't. He was tired, that's all.

He poured himself a drink. Night was already falling over the harbor, the lights on the marina glittering like earthbound stars. Where did she live? In Old Port, with its handsome brick buildings and cobblestone streets? Or west of here, nearer to the clinic?

Was she thinking about him? Or had she already put him out of her mind, an incident that had happened and wouldn't be repeated?

He loathed the thought of being so summarily dismissed. Forgotten, like a garment she'd discarded.

Travis went to bed early, slept badly for the third night in a row and did a ten-hour shift at the hospital the next day. Afterward, changed into jeans and a T-shirt, he went to the grocery store nearest the medical center. He could have eaten out; but he'd tired of that in his first month here, and now preferred to cook something back at the condo. He was frowning at the array of steaks, wondering if he'd barbecue on the balcony, when a woman's voice said, "Travis? It is you, isn't it?"

He turned, recognizing the voice almost immediately. "Trish," he said warmly, "how are you? Long time no see."

"Eleven or twelve years," she said, shifting the carton of milk she was carrying to shake his hand.

She'd changed very little in those years, her long blond hair still in an untidy knot on her head, her eyes the same warm brown. Travis had been engaged to her his final year at medical school; for a moment he felt like that young man again, head stuffed with knowledge, wanderlust tugging him like a magnet even as he was pulled toward the more ordinary longings for home and a family. He said impulsively, "Have you got time for a drink? Or dinner?"

She consulted her watch. "A drink. I'm going to my in-laws for dinner, my husband's out of town and they've been looking after the children for me. Let me just pay for this."

He grabbed a steak, a few onions and some broccoli, and followed her. Ten minutes later they were seated in a booth in a nearby pub. "To chance meetings," Travis said, raising his glass. "Tell me about your husband...and how many children?"

"I have photos," she grinned, and showed him snapshots of two towheaded little boys and an angelic little girl, all blond curls and dimples. Her husband, Tom, was tall and athletic, with a pleasant smile. All five looked happy together, Travis thought. As though they fit.

"You're fortunate," he said. "A lovely family, Trish."

"And you? Have you married?"

He shifted in the seat. "Never have, no. I've spent most of my time overseas since you and I broke up. You name it, I've been there."

"It wouldn't be easy to meet women when you're on the move a lot, I suppose."

"You can always meet women if you want to."

"So you're still unattached," she said slowly. "Do you remember what I said to you the night I broke our engagement?"

"That you wanted a man who was head over heels in love with you," he said promptly. "Is Tom like that?"

Her face softened. "Yes. Even after three kids and the usual ups and downs of marriage. I lucked out."

"You knew enough to wait for the real thing." With an urgency that took him by surprise, Travis asked, "Did you know the minute you met Tom? Or was it more gradual?"

She took a sip of her martini. "After you left, and even though I was sure I'd done the right thing by breaking up with you, I was lonely. So I got a dog at the animal shelter, kind of an ugly dog actually, that no one else wanted to adopt. I was walking him in Deering Park one evening by the pond when he started to play with a very patrician collie. He fell in love with the collie and I fell in love with the collie's owner. And yes, I knew right away. I can tell you what Tom was wearing that evening and what we said, and how alive I felt. Utterly and wonderfully alive."

"And it's lasted…"

"As I say, we lucked out. It doesn't last for everyone,

Travis. But you have to be willing to take the risk. And in the rough times to work your heart out.''

Moodily he stared into his Scotch. The moment Julie had stood up on the wharf and turned to face him, hadn't he in some primal sense recognized her?

"You've met someone," Trish ventured.

"Not really." He let a mouthful of the liquor slide down his throat, Julie's face in his mind's eye as clearly as if she were actually standing there.

"Come clean," Trish said pithily.

Exasperated with himself, Travis said, "I met this woman last Friday, you're right, and my hormones have been in an uproar ever since. But that's all it is. Lust."

"If it's lust, anyone will do."

He didn't want anyone. He wanted Julie. But it was still lust.

"One of the things I always admired about you was your honesty," Trish remarked. "You said it like it was. Surely you haven't lost that?"

"She's got me so riled up, I don't know what the truth is!"

"Maybe you've fallen in love with her."

He made an instinctive gesture of repudiation. "I don't know what love is, Trish…didn't you accuse me of that all those years ago?"

"I did, yes. You'd get just so close to me and then you'd back off. I was younger then and I had the world figured out, so I accused you of being afraid of intimacy. You'd lost your mother and you'd decided at the age of six that you weren't going to trust any female ever again." Her smile was rueful. "I wouldn't be quite so frank now. Or so sure that I was right."

"You probably were right, though. My mother disappeared between one day and the next. I don't remember the funeral, or any of the relatives visiting. I do know my dad would never allow her name to be mentioned. And then I was shipped off to boarding school as though nothing had happened. Two years later he married Corinne.''

"Little wonder you're afraid to trust. But if this woman is the right one, Travis, she's worth fighting for. Love's worth fighting for, that's what I'm saying. And now I'm going to shut up, and you're going to tell me about some of your adventures overseas.''

Travis dredged his memory for events both touching and funny; and half an hour later they left the pub. Trish reached up and kissed him on the cheek. "It was lovely to see you again. Good luck, Travis. Keep in touch and make sure you bring her to dinner to meet the family.''

"Don't hold your breath," he said, and watched her leave. Not for the first time, he thought how wise a woman she was. He was glad she was happy.

He was even more glad she'd had the strength of character to break their engagement. He hadn't been in love with her, not really. He'd never fallen in love in his life. Now that he was alone, he could admit something else: while he'd had all the normal sexual urges for Trish of a man in his early twenties, he'd never been pulled to her the way he was to Julie.

But to suggest he'd fallen for Julie was ridiculous.

The condo seemed even more empty after seeing Trish's snapshots. Was this what he wanted for the rest of his life, Travis wondered, putting the bag of groceries down on the kitchen counter. A series of temporary lodgings; and no one to welcome him when he came home at the end of the day.

He'd always prided himself on his self-sufficiency. His independence.

Doggedly Travis cooked the steak and watched the late news. He worked several extra shifts that week, as well as volunteering at a local clinic. He also found out Julie's phone number, although he didn't call her. But he thought about her most of the time, far too much for his peace of mind. When the telephone rang on Friday evening, he raced to pick it up, absurdly certain that Julie would be on the other end of the line.

"Bryce here, Travis. How you doing, buddy?"

Normally Travis was glad to hear from Bryce; but tonight he had to swallow disappointment bitter as gall. "Fine...how are you and where are you?"

The last question was always relevant: apart from being a self-made millionaire and Travis's best friend, Bryce Laribee was an international consultant in computer programming who traveled the world over. "Bangkok. Hotter 'n hell. I'm heading for Hanoi tomorrow. You getting itchy feet yet?"

Bryce had been convinced Travis wouldn't last more than three weeks in Portland, Maine. "The practice is okay. I'm doing some freeby stuff in a downtown clinic as well."

"I knew it," Bryce chuckled. "Where are you headed come September?"

"I've got a couple of prospects. Mexico, near Cuernavaca. Or Honduras...any chance of us connecting this summer?"

"Give me a month. Then I should be back in the States." Bryce paused. "You mentioned you might try to get together with your father—did anything come of that?"

Briefly Travis described the party and the rather puzzling reconciliation with Charles. "It was all too slick, too easy. And for some reason he wants me out of Portland on the first flight. I can't think why."

"Sounds like your father has all the instincts of a Machiavelli without the brains," Bryce said caustically. "But you're not planning on leaving?"

"No. I guess not."

Bryce, who'd grown up in the slums of Boston, was

known for directness. ''What's up? Did this really bother you? You don't sound like yourself.''

Travis hesitated. ''I met a woman.''

''You meet lots of women. They trample each other to get to you first, you think I haven't noticed that?''

Travis grinned into the telephone. ''You're not backward in that department yourself.''

''So what's with this woman?''

''If I knew that, I wouldn't be sitting in this goddamned condo all by myself on a Friday night!''

There was a small silence. ''Give, buddy.''

There was no one Travis trusted as much as his old friend Bryce. At the age of twelve, Bryce had been admitted as a scholarship student to the boarding school Travis had been attending for six years. In Bryce's first week, Travis had saved him from certain explusion at least three times; then, together, they'd put the fear of God in the four bullies who'd been terrorizing the dorms after dark. Travis said, smiling, ''Remember Jed Cathcart, the look on his face when you dumped that bucket of spaghetti all over him?''

''And then we wiped the floor with him and the spaghetti. Those were the days, Travis. Things were simpler, you knew who the bad guys were...now tell me about this woman. Name, age and vital statistics.''

Stumbling at first, but gathering momentum as he went, Travis told the whole story, from the stormy meeting on the wharf to the equally stormy goodbye in her bedroom. ''So that's that,'' he ended. ''I've never chased a woman in my life and I'm not starting with her. Wouldn't do me any good, anyway.''

''So why aren't you dating that nurse you told me about? The one with the big blue eyes. Sounded like she'd be willing.''

Travis had had a coffee with the nurse on his Wednesday

shift; he could have asked her out then. "Too tall, too blond, wrong shape, you want me to go on?"

"You've got it bad, man."

"I'll get over it."

"You in love with this Julie?"

"No!"

"Not in the habit of falling in love myself, so I wouldn't know the symptoms. But it's not like you to pine like a lovesick teenager over a female who's given you nothing but grief. You know what you should do?" Bryce didn't wait for Travis to answer. "Call her up. Or better still, find out where she lives and knock on her door. See her again. Maybe you'll find out you've imagined the whole thing. So she's got green eyes. So what? Cats have got green eyes and you don't want to date a cat."

"She's as graceful as a cat. And just as self-contained."

"She's got claws, too." Bryce's voice roughened. "No broad's going to mess up your life, Travis, not if I have anything to say about it."

"You think if I saw her, I'd be over it?"

"Worth a try. Or maybe she'll have changed her mind and jump your bones."

"In my dreams."

"What have you got to lose? You're as cranky as a caged hyena."

"You got that part right." Travis grimaced. "Not that a second rejection'll make me feel any better."

"Don't be such a defeatist! Women drool all over you, I've watched 'em. Go for it, Travis. I'll call you next week and see what happened."

A few minutes later Travis rang off. He wasn't going to go and see Julie. If she didn't want him, that was her loss.

On which militant note, he went to bed.

CHAPTER NINE

ON SUNDAY afternoon it poured with rain. This suited Julie's mood. Her parents were coming for dinner and it would take her the rest of the afternoon to get ready. Her mother was a fanatic housekeeper. But why, thought Julie, as she wielded the dust cloth, did she think she had to clean her apartment from top to bottom before her mother could walk in the door? Was she still that much under Pearl Renshaw's thumb?

Julie loved her little apartment, which was owned by a wealthy and eccentric widow at the clinic whose arthritic pain she'd been able to relieve. She was paying through the nose for it, but it was only for a couple more months and her savings account was decidedly healthy at the moment.

She was living by the waterfront, on the top floor of an old brick building near the marina. She'd filled her tiny balcony with flowering plants, bought some attractive hand-painted furniture, and arranged some of her collection of artifacts from her travels on the walls. It felt like home.

Or it had, until she came back from Manatuck.

With a ferocious energy that had nothing to do with her mother, Julie scoured the tub until it gleamed. She wasn't going to think about Manatuck. Or Travis. Or the fact that her body, awakened by Travis, now refused to go back to sleep.

She'd read about desire in books. Even though she'd felt twinges of it now and then with one or the other of the men she'd dated, she'd concluded privately that the authors had overactive imaginations. She'd never been obsessed by a man, so that he haunted her sleep, her dreams and her daylight hours.

Never, until this last week.

Scrubbing the bathroom floor as sexual sublimation, she thought with an unhappy smile, and carried the bucket into the kitchen. Her knee still hurt. Another reminder of a time she desperately wanted to forget.

Her bedroom was immaculate, the bathroom pristine, and it only took a few minutes to tidy, dust and vacuum the living room and dining area. Which left the kitchen.

The rain was hammering on the skylight and streaming down the windows; she could scarcely see the harbor. A ginger ale. That's what she needed. And then she'd tackle the kitchen. She'd made a cheesecake this morning, so that much was done. As for the rest, she was planning a rather complicated Moroccan chicken dish that she'd organize once she'd finished cleaning.

At least work had gone well this week, that was one thing to be grateful for. She was finding the clinic a welcome respite from her normal work; she hadn't realized how stressful her overseas contracts had been until she'd come home to Portland for the summer. Besides, some of her clients were a delight. There was Abigail Masters who'd found her this apartment, who smoked cigars and swore like a stevedore; Leonora Connolly, a retired dancer who was paying the physical price for her career with humor and grace; and Malcolm McAdams, a famous hybridizer of daylilies, who insisted on bringing his Manx cat to his sessions.

It was such a change from crushing heat, foreign tongues and equally crushing poverty...

Julie was just topping up the glass with pop when her buzzer sounded. She frowned. The little boy downstairs had a tendency to open the security door to whomever he pleased; she must speak to his parents about it. Again. She went to the door, peering through the peephole.

Travis was standing in the hallway. The glass jerked in her hand, spilling ginger ale on her shirt. She looked down at herself. Bare feet, a luridly bruised gash on her leg, cutoff shorts and her very oldest shirt which had a button missing in a rather strategic place.

Let him see her as she was. That should fix him.

She pulled the door open. His hair was plastered to his skull, his raincoat was dripping on the mat, and his eyes were even more blue than she remembered. He was carrying a rather bedraggled bouquet of sweetpeas. She went on the attack. "How did you find out where I live?"

"Asked one of my colleagues at Silversides."

"How did you get in the front door?"

"A kid with bright red hair let me in. You should complain about that."

"I have. His parents think he's a little angel who couldn't possibly be breaking the rules."

"Are you going to ask me in?"

Her heart was bouncing around in her chest, her knees were weak and her mouth dry. Too much adrenaline, she thought clinically. "Give me one good reason why I should."

"Because you want to," Travis said.

She wanted to kiss him senseless, Julie thought faintly. If only she'd taken yesterday's newspaper to the little coffee shop on the corner instead of opting for ginger ale in her messy kitchen. "You're wet," she said with blinding originality.

"It's raining. Or hadn't you noticed?"

So what was she going to say? You can come in if you promise to stay at least six feet away from me at all times? "I'm cleaning," she said. "I'm a mess."

Travis looked her up and down, taking his time about it,

laughter lurking in his eyes. As warm color crept up her cheeks, he said, "Are you last on the list?"

"After the kitchen."

He eyed the glass in her hand. "I like ginger ale."

As all her nerves screamed danger, she gave him what she hoped was a noncommittal smile. "You'd better come in. Here, give me your coat and I'll hang it in the closet."

Once she'd done so, he handed her the flowers. "These are for you. They were selling them at the market."

She frequently went to the market, which was only a few blocks from her apartment. "Where do you live?" she said, suddenly suspicious.

He crossed the living room, rubbing at the pane. "You should be able to see my place from here. The second group of condos."

On a clear day she'd be in full sight of his windows, she thought edgily. Just what she needed. "Do you really want pop? I could make you some coffee. Or there's beer."

"A ginger ale would be fine."

She fled to the tiny galley kitchen, where unwashed dishes were heaped on the counter. After rinsing the worst of the stain from her shirt, she filled a second glass and went back into the living room. Travis was standing on the sisal mat, looking around him with appreciation. He dwarfed the room; he also looked very much at home.

"Those carvings, aren't they from Bali?" She nodded. "And the pillows look like they came from a Calcutta bazaar."

"They did."

"You've traveled a lot."

She said rapidly, "I do overseas contracts all the time. I just came home this summer because my mother had a minor heart attack."

He picked up a delicately carved giraffe she'd bought in Tanzania. "Where have you worked?" After she'd rattled off the names of some of the countries, he added, "You didn't tell me any of this."

"I don't often talk about what I do. It makes people uncomfortable."

"So you've noticed that, too...you see, I do the same sort of thing." Travis named the international organization he'd worked for the last ten years, establishing that he'd left Tanzania the year before Julie had arrived.

She frowned at him. "I thought you were a rich doctor who looked after the rich."

"And I thought you catered to the privileged and pampered."

"You know the kind of things people think. Do-gooder with a savior complex."

"Guilt-dumpers. Disturbers of the status quo."

"Weirdos, wackos and neurotics."

He gave her a warm smile. "It's not easy work, is it, Julie?"

His smile made her tingle all the way from her head to her bare toes. "No," she muttered. "No, it's not. Would you like some more pop?"

"Sure." As she padded into the kitchen, he followed her. "I'll help you with the dishes."

If he'd dwarfed the living room, he filled the kitchen. Almost dizzy with longing, Julie picked up the sweet peas and buried her face in them. "They're my favorite flower," she mumbled.

He put down his glass on the counter. "It's interesting that we do the same kind of work...means we share a basic value system."

"So what?" she blurted.

"One more thing we have in common."

"You're playing games with me, Travis."

"Okay—I'll cut to the chase. Do you know why I'm here?"

She looked at him warily. "Not really."

"Then I'll tell you. I've thought about you all week, night and day. I'll be honest—I figured if I came here today and saw you again, I'd realize that you weren't anything special, that I'd been fooling myself."

She looked down at herself with a shaky grin. "You've got your proof. In spades."

"It wouldn't matter what you wore or how you looked," he said with suppressed violence. "The moment you answered the door, I knew nothing had changed."

She found she was gripping the edge of the counter with bruising strength, mostly to keep herself from pulling his head down and kissing him until neither one of them could breathe. She said carefully, "What exactly are you saying?"

"Hell, I don't know." He ran his fingers through his damp hair. "I want you as much now as I wanted you on Manatuck. I guess that's what I'm saying."

The intensity in his face made her tremble. She reached past him for the pop bottle, inadvertently brushing his bare forearm with her own. The pop was forgotten. Her hand stopped in midair. Then, very slowly, she lowered it to lie on his arm. She closed her eyes, oblivious to everything but his nearness and a tumult of longing. All those authors were right, she thought. Desire does exist. It's like fire, hot and urgent and leapingly alive.

In a strangled voice Travis said, "Julie..."

His arms went around her. She buried her face in his shoulder, inhaling the clean masculine scent of his skin, so very much a part of him, so uniquely his. Then, of her own accord, she looked up, took his face between her palms and kissed him full on the mouth. As she'd been wanting to do ever since he'd arrived.

She'd learned a thing or two about kissing on Manatuck. But just in case he doubted her intentions, she whispered in between fierce, heated kisses, "Make love to me, Travis. Now."

"There's nothing I want more in the world," he said, kissing her back with such blatant hunger that her body melted into his. Then, awkwardly because the kitchen was so small, he picked her up. "Don't kick the pop bottle," he added, his eyes giving her a very different message.

His eyes were undressing her. Against her cheek she felt the hard pounding of his heart, under her knees the sinewy strength of his arm. As he edged out of the kitchen, she said, "Down the hall on the right," and added with a tiny chuckle, "it's not usually so tidy."

Because the room was small, she'd bought a three-quarter spindle bed, covering it with an old-fashioned quilt. Not bothering to pull the quilt back, Travis laid her down on the bed and covered her with his big body, his weight on his elbows. She was trembling very lightly. Then his head swooped down like a falcon to the prey, his mouth plundering hers until she was nothing but an ache of passionate need.

Only then did Travis reach for the top button on her shirt. His fingers brushed her skin; his irises were a blazing blue. Straddling her, he eased her arms out of the shirt, then in the same intent silence undid her bra, tossing it to the floor. She said softly, "Take your shirt off, Travis."

His hands weren't quite steady as he fumbled with the buttons, and this, more than anything, touched Julie to the heart. Travis, she already knew, was a man both self-contained and very much in control of himself: that she should make him lose that control filled her with a confusing mixture of wonder and excitement. Very deliberately she reached for the zipper on her shorts, easing them down her hips, then kicking them to the floor. She said with a faint grin, "Because I always wear utilitarian cotton in the tropics, I go overboard on lace when I'm home."

"Black lace," he said huskily. Then with sudden impatience, he stripped off his slacks and briefs.

She wriggled out of the black lace. "Watch out for my knee, it's still sore," she said, and pulled his head down, her tongue darting to meet his in a kiss that seemed to last forever. A kiss in which the old Julie vanished.

The new Julie, not knowing quite what to expect yet utterly willing to find out, tugged at Travis's shoulders. "Lie on top of me," she begged, "I want to feel every inch of you."

He slid his mouth down her throat, finding her breast, his hips pressing her into the quilt. She wrapped her arms around him, glorying in his weight, crying out with pleasure as he laved her nipple with his tongue. Sensation lanced through her, fiery and imperative. With a sensuality she had never thought she possessed, she ran her fingers through his chest hair, tugging at it gently, following it all the way to his navel and then beyond.

Briefly he lifted his hips. And then she found his center, hot and silky, infinitely desirable. He groaned deep in his throat as she touched him, burying his face in her shoulder, his heart pounding against her ribs. As though he couldn't help himself, he eased her legs apart and plunged into her.

She gasped with delight, welcoming him and gathering him in. Inexpertly she moved her hips until he filled her, so that she scarcely knew where she ended and he began. Her own rhythms seized her, urgently and inexorably, mounting toward an unbearable peak. "Travis," she muttered, "oh Travis…"

"Sweetheart…" he said roughly, his fierce thrusts pushing her over the edge, the hard plane of his chest inflaming her nipples until she arched to meet him, crying out his name in an avalanche of release. He convulsed within her, his own cry echoing in her ears. Then he collapsed on top of her.

Julie lay very still, and for several minutes couldn't have said a word to save her soul. Gradually she came back to herself, to two hearts racing as one and a feeling of peace and fulfillment such as she'd never known. I've come home, she thought. It's taken me all these years and many thousands of miles, and now I've come home...

Abruptly Travis raised his head. "Julie, I'm sorry—that was over before it began."

A slow smile spread across Julie's face. "You're sorry?" she said. "I hope not. But maybe I'm the one who should be apologizing. I was so impatient, so demanding—in such a big hurry. I wanted you so much, I couldn't bear to wait."

Travis gave a sudden exultant laugh. "How about we both forget the word *sorry?* And how about we do it again? Say in five minutes. And this time maybe both of us can restrain ourselves so that it lasts longer than five minutes."

"You were timing us?" she said, batting her lashes at him.

"Not exactly. Too much else was going on. As you may have noticed."

"Who, me?" Julie chuckled. She'd never known laughter could be part of lovemaking. She was beginning to suspect that there was a lot she'd never known. Letting all her newfound wonderment show in her face, she said ingenuously, "So I'm supposed to kiss you with restraint? Is that the way it works?"

"No," he said, "you're supposed to kiss me like this."

He bent his head, finding her mouth, moving his lips over hers with tantalizing lightness. His tongue sought out hers, dancing with it, advancing and retreating. And at the same time, with exquisite pressure, he was stroking the warm slope of her breast, again and again.

Low in her belly, a deep, sweet ache was born. She had

time. That was what Travis was saying. Time to savor every sensation. Time to learn his body, to discover what he liked and what pleased him.

Was that what was meant by intimacy?

CHAPTER TEN

JULIE brought her hands to Travis's face, searching out the hard planes of his jaw and cheekbones, tracing his deepset eyes, her own smiling into his with a mixture of shyness and invitation. His hair, so thick and silky; the corded tendons in his neck; the dip of his collarbone and the swell of taut muscle that was his shoulder, she explored them all and found them all utterly entrancing. And the whole time she watched his face, losing herself in the brilliant blue depths of his eyes. He said unsteadily, "Have I told you yet today how beautiful you are?"

"If you did, I missed it."

"How your eyes are the green of a hummingbird's wings? How your skin is smooth as a river?" As he ran his hands down her body, she shivered in response, his voice casting a spell over her. "How you tremble when I touch you. Like this. Or like this."

His palms, curving to her hips, cupping her buttocks, then sliding to her inner thighs, did indeed fill her with a wild, sweet trembling. Tears suddenly blurred her vision. "No one's ever said such beautiful things to me."

He found the sleek petals of flesh between her legs, seeking out their heart, watching her face change as he stroked her very gently. "Does that give you pleasure?"

She thrust with her hips, briefly closing her eyes. "Yes, oh yes…"

She was drowning in desire, flooded by its tides. And she'd been ignorant enough to think it didn't exist. She knew better now. Desire existed. Desire for Travis, for his big, muscular body and all the wonderful things he was doing to her.

Going on instinct, Julie moved her hands further down his body, roaming the corded muscles of his belly, the jut of hipbone and his taut flanks. "If I'm beautiful," she murmured, "so are you."

He suddenly rolled over, carrying her with him so that she was lying on top of him, pulling her face down to kiss her again. And all the time he was exploring her breasts and narrow waist, the flare of her hips, in slow, sensuous strokes. She kissed him back, moving his thighs apart so she could rub herself against him with a matching sensuality. "Do you like that?" she asked.

"Like it?" he gasped. "Julie, I love everything you do."

With sudden shyness she said, "You mean I don't disappoint you?"

His hands stilled. "You couldn't be further from the truth." He paused for a moment, as if searching for the right words. "You told me you'd made love a long time ago, that you weren't a virgin…but it's almost as though I am the first. There's an innocence about you that makes me feel very special."

She wasn't sure she liked the direction he was heading. "I'm doing my best to lose that innocence," she said lightly, "which will require your full cooperation."

"You've got it," Travis said, and lifted her to ride him.

She was more than ready for him; as he buried himself deep within her, she gasped with delight. Again Travis found the place where she was most achingly sensitive, teasing her flesh until she was shuddering with pent-up need, her head thrown back, her belly taut within the hollow of her rib cage. An inward throbbing seized her, wild as an ocean storm; she rode him as though he were the waves of the sea until the last barriers between them dissolved, and his own climax reared to meet hers.

The last fierce ripple ran through her; the sounds she was hearing were her own harsh indrawn breaths mingled with his. As though she were boneless, she sank down on top of him, holding him close, his body hair rough under her cheek. "It happened again," she said raggedly.

"I feel like I'm making up for a lifetime of hunger," Travis said hoarsely, wrapping his arms around her.

"I feel like I've been ambushed," she croaked. "I had no idea making love could be like that."

"Look at me, Julie."

She glanced up, the expression on his face catching at her heartstrings. Distantly she felt the stirrings of what was unquestionably panic. "Travis, I—"

"I want you to know something—I've never made love like that in my life," he said in the same hoarse voice. "I'd pictured seducing you slowly, taking my time, giving you the most pleasure I was capable of. But instead, both times, I was totally out of control. That's not like me...to lose myself like that."

Her one desire to defuse a level of emotion that terrified her, Julie said pertly, "It's not like me, either—you can take that to the bank."

To her relief he smiled. "We could try again. Although we may have to wait more than five minutes this time...I'm only human." His smile widened. "Tell you what. Why don't I take you out for dinner? Then we could come back here and make love all night. Or we could go to my place if you like."

"Dinner...did you say *dinner?*" In a flurry of bare limbs, Julie sat bolt upright, her face horror-stricken. "Moroccan chicken. Ohmigosh!"

"What's the matter?" Travis demanded. As she tried to scramble off him, he grabbed her by the wrist. "Surely the thought of a dinner date with me isn't that horrendous?"

She tugged futilely at his grasp. "My parents, they're

coming here for dinner. I'm making this fancy chicken casserole.'' Her gaze fell on the bedside clock, her voice rising. ''They're going to arrive in three-quarters of an hour.''

Travis said promptly, ''I'll do the dishes, and you cook.''

She looked at him as though he had two heads. ''Are you suggesting you stay for dinner with my parents?''

''Yeah...I guess I am.''

''No way! I'm not letting them within a mile of you. Let go, Travis, *please*.''

If anything, his grip tightened. ''What's the big deal with your parents, Julie?''

She struck at his hand. ''I am not going to tell you my life history when my mother and father will be ringing the doorbell in exactly forty-three minutes.'' She gave a moan of despair. ''They're always punctual. Precisely on time. They'll take one look at me and they'll know what I've been doing all afternoon. How could I have forgotten they were coming?''

''You forgot because we were doing something more important.''

How could she argue with him? She was the one who'd thrown herself at him. ''That's your interpretation,'' she said fractiously.

Travis released her wrist so suddenly that she almost fell sideways. ''You want me out of here? Right now?''

''Of course!''

His voice hardened. ''There's no *of course* about it. Not from my point of view. We just made love. Twice, in case you've forgotten. And now you want to hustle me out the door so your parents won't catch sight of me and think you've actually been with a man. How old are you, for heaven's sake?''

''Thirty,'' she muttered, scrabbling for her clothes, which seemed to be scattered all over the floor. ''What's that got to do with it? Do hurry, Travis.''

"Just you wait a minute," he said grimly. He stood up, towering over her, stark naked and angrier than she'd ever seen him. Taking her by the shoulders, he grated, "We made love. That means something to me, and I'm not going to walk out the door as though it never happened. We'll get together tomorrow evening after work. We can meet in the middle of the park, or in a coffee shop, or all the way out at the Spring Point lighthouse—I don't give a damn where we meet. But we're going to meet. And you're going to talk, Julie. You're going to tell me why you've never had a serious boyfriend in your life, and how that relates to your parents. Have you got that?"

It wasn't easy to be cool, calm and collected when wearing nothing but black lace briefs and confronted by a large, angry and entirely naked male; but Julie did her best. "That's your agenda," she said coldly. "You haven't asked me mine."

"I don't care if you've already got plans—cancel them," he grated, and with complete composure bent to pick up his scattered clothes. Julie averted her eyes from the long curve of his spine. She still wanted him, she thought, appalled. How could she? What was wrong with her?

Was she some kind of sex maniac?

An inner resolve, scarcely articulated, hardened into shape. "I—I don't think we should see each other again," she said.

Travis's hands stilled on his belt buckle. "Would you mind repeating that?"

"You heard."

"We've just been as intimate as a man and woman can be, and now you want me to vanish from your life?"

Chilled to the bone, Julie wrapped her arms around her waist. "Yes," she said, "I do."

His eyes never leaving her face, Travis reached for his

shirt. "You don't think two people should be involved in that decision?"

Flinching from his sarcasm, she said, "It's precisely because I don't want to be part of a couple that I'm making the decision."

"Do you have to sound so cold-blooded?"

He sounded anything but. Unbidden, an image of his face at the moment of climax flashed into her mind. Julie shoved it away, pain lancing her heart. "I'm trying to avoid disappointment in the future," she cried. "For both of us."

"You let me look after myself," Travis said grimly. "You're looking for guarantees, Julie, that's what you're doing. There aren't any, haven't you learned that yet?"

"I won't commit to any kind of long-term relationship with you...so what's the point of seeing you again? We'll both end up getting hurt."

"I don't understand—you've lived in India and Tanzania, yet you won't take the smallest of gambles in your personal life. What kind of parents have you got?"

"The kind that are a perfect advertisement for singlehood," she flared. "Travis, I have the right to say I don't want to see you again, and I'm exercising that right."

Doing up the buttons on his shirt, he said, "You're denying yourself the possibility of falling in love, of marriage and bearing children...is that the way you plan to live for the rest of your life?"

"The first time we met, you told me it was against your principles to belong to anyone!"

"Maybe I've changed," he said.

"Then that's your problem." She had to end this. "It would have been better if this afternoon had never happened, I was a fool to even let you in the door."

"You were the one who instigated our lovemaking."

"I made a mistake!"

"So an experience that damn near knocked me off my feet was nothing but a mistake?"

"Stop it! I can't take any more of this. Just go away and leave me alone, Travis—that's all I ask."

"You don't have a worry in the world," he said savagely, turned on his heel and left the bedroom.

Julie opened her closet door, grabbing a skirt and blouse off the hangers. She was trembling again, just as she'd trembled when Travis had undressed her. But now it was nothing to do with desire.

Dimly, as if the sounds came from another world, she heard Travis's shoes scrape on the front mat; then the apartment door slammed shut.

He'd gone.

She'd done the right thing. She knew she had. Yet all she wanted to do was throw herself across the bed and cry her eyes out. In the space of a few minutes, she'd plummeted from the bliss she'd found in his arms to this dead despair.

For it had been bliss. She'd felt whole, perhaps for the first time in her life. Travis had made her complete.

With a tiny moan of dismay, Julie ran for the bathroom and turned on the shower. Ten minutes later, dressed and more or less presentable, she hurried into the kitchen. She'd scrap making the Moroccan chicken. She had time to do the dishes, run a mop over the kitchen floor and thaw some pasta sauce that she had in the freezer. Thank heavens she'd made the cheesecake this morning.

Before all this had happened. Before her life had changed irreversibly.

Quickly Julie filled the sink with hot water. She mustn't think about Travis; she couldn't afford to. She squirted detergent into the sink and tossed in the dirty cutlery; when the buzzer sounded twenty minutes later, the clean dishes were stacked in the tray, the kitchen floor had dried, she'd added extra scallops and shrimp to the sauce and she'd just thrown the place mats on the table. The other thing she'd done was bury the sweet peas Travis had brought her in the depths of the garbage can.

Taking a long, deep breath, Julie walked to the door, opening it wide. "Hello Mum, Dad," she said, and lifted her cheek to be kissed. Her parents didn't do hugs.

"Hello, Julie," her mother said. "You look very flushed, are you feeling all right?"

"Of course she is," her father said heartily. "You're like me, never ill. Right, Julie?"

This was a not-so-subtle dig at his wife Pearl, who enjoyed a variety of ailments, many of them genuine. The minor heart attack she'd had in the spring had been lumped with everything else by her husband; Julie, more knowledgeable, had been encouraging her mother to eat a little less and exercise a little more.

Pearl ignored her husband's comment, passing Julie her wet raincoat. "What a terrible day...oh, you didn't get around to laying the table?"

How well Julie knew that air of faint reproach; all too often it had been directed her way. "A friend dropped in unexpectedly," she said, opting for a censored version of the truth. "So I'm not quite ready."

Her mother headed right for the kitchen. "Seafood pasta, how nice...you've heard they've been having trouble with the local scallops, have you? Some kind of algal growth."

"No, I hadn't heard," Julie said evenly. "Can I get you a glass of wine?"

"I'll stick to fruit juice, dear. Much better for you."

"Do you know why the French live longer?" Thomas Renshaw interposed. "Red wine, proven to cut down on heart attacks."

Julie said dryly, "I've only got white, Dad."

"If you'd had red, he'd have wanted white," Pearl said with a merry little laugh. "Wouldn't you, darling?"

Julie winced. "Speaking of heart attacks, how are you feeling, Mum?"

Pearl discussed her cholesterol level, her blood pressure monitor and the new cardiologist she'd seen last week. "Such a sweet man, I should introduce you to him, Julie."

Julie didn't want to meet another doctor. "You've had your hair done, it looks nice."

"It didn't turn out at all the color I wanted. I'll just have to change salons again."

"Are there any you haven't tried?" Thomas said, accepting a glass of wine. "I can't see what the big fuss is all about."

"When you had a full head of hair, you used to fret every time the barber cut it," Pearl remarked.

This was a double blow, for Thomas hated being almost bald; and was still fussy about how the remnant was cut. Julie turned away, taking knives and forks out of the drawer. "Would you mind putting these out, Dad? And the candlesticks are on the coffee table...it's almost dark enough to light them, isn't it?"

She was exhausted already, she thought unhappily, taking some rolls out of the bread box and turning on the oven to heat them. Then she bent to find the ingredients for a tossed salad from the bottom shelf of the refrigerator. Pearl took advantage of her husband's temporary absence to say, "Your father doesn't look well, but he refuses to go to the doctor...you just don't know what I have to put up with."

"You're not backward about telling me, Mum."

Pearl gave a theatrical sigh. "Well, you're my only child, who else can I tell?"

Do you love your husband? The question hovered on the tip of Julie's tongue. Exasperated with herself, she bit it back. What was the point of asking? For as long as she could remember, Thomas and Pearl had existed in an outwardly polite state of constant warfare. No overt anger, no attempt to solve their differences; just an incessant sniping at each other that Julie loathed. There were lines of discontent in her mother's carefully made-up face; her father's faded hazel eyes held neither hope nor laughter. She said with attempted cheer, "I made a fabulous cheesecake for dessert, you'll like it."

"Too many calories, I'm sure."

"You worry them off faster than you put them on," Julie teased. "Anyway, I used low-fat ingredients."

"When you've been married as long as I have, you have to keep up your appearance," Pearl said. "The pasta's boiling over, Julie."

Julie turned the heat down, set the timer and slung chopped tomatoes in the salad bowl. Luckily she had some homemade dressing left. Ten minutes later, they sat down to eat; her parents, as she'd learned long ago, didn't believe in dining after six-thirty.

The candles flickered light and shadow on the ceiling, and rain streaked the windowpanes. Pearl said, "I really must make you some curtains, Julie, anyone can look in."

"I'm three stories up…besides, I'll be gone in a couple of months, it's not worth it." She smiled at her mother. "But thanks for the offer."

"Oh, of course, you're leaving before winter…the older I get, the more I dread the winters. I miss you so much when you're overseas, dear."

I won't move back to Portland, I won't, Julie thought frantically, and felt guilt curdle her stomach. She should be a better daughter: closer to home, more involved. But she'd lived with her parents until she was nearly eighteen, and her presence hadn't made either of them any happier. In fact, the opposite had been true: their daughter had given them one more thing to argue about.

The cheesecake caused Thomas to complain that Pearl never made desserts, and Pearl to calculate how many calories he'd just devoured. Julie poured coffee, listening to the rain beat against the windows. What would Travis have thought of her parents? Had he met them, would he have understood why she'd sent him away?

"You're spilling the coffee," Pearl said sharply.

"Oh...sorry, I'll get a cloth."

"You don't seem yourself," Thomas said. "Is there anything you're not telling us?"

Oh, yes, Julie thought wildly. There's plenty. Starting with this afternoon, when I just about attacked a man I scarcely know and behaved like a wanton hussy in the bed just down the hall. *Wanton hussy* was a phrase she'd heard her father use about a woman in a television play. Which, as Pearl had pointed out, he'd watched right to the end. Julie said carefully, "I'm a little tired, that's all."

"I don't know why you had to take that job all summer," her mother said. "You could have spent more time with us."

"I can use the money," Julie said mildly. "More coffee, Dad?"

After dinner Pearl insisted on washing the dishes, they all watched a nature show, and then her parents left. Julie closed the door behind them and wandered back into the living room. Maybe she should have let Travis stay for dinner, she thought wretchedly. Wouldn't that have been the easiest way to show him why she was so dead-set against commitment? She'd once suggested to her mother that if Pearl was so unhappy, maybe she should get a divorce; affronted, Pearl had lectured her about the sanctity of marriage vows, the tribulations of a woman's lot and the lifelong duties of motherhood. Julie had never mentioned divorce again.

Restlessly she roamed the apartment. She couldn't go for

a walk, it was still pouring rain. She couldn't vacuum the apartment, it was already clean. And she couldn't sleep on the couch, the cushions were too thin. She forced herself to walk into her bedroom, get undressed and get into bed. But when she turned her head to the pillow, she caught, elusively, the clean male scent of Travis's body. Her fists clenched, Julie fought back tears that if they once started might never stop. She'd made the right choice, the only possible choice, by sending Travis away.

Hold that thought, Julie.

Closing her eyes, she started counting parakeets, which she'd long ago decided was a more colorful way of getting to sleep than counting sheep.

But it was a long time before her strategy worked.

CHAPTER ELEVEN

THE evenings home alone in her apartment were the worst. By Tuesday evening, Julie had it figured out: subconsciously, and despite the fact that she was the one who'd sent Travis packing, she was expecting him to get in touch with her.

Her mother phoned. So did Kathy, one of the nurses from the clinic, and her hairdresser. Travis didn't phone.

Why would he? She'd told him, unequivocally, to get lost. But to her horror, she realized she was furious with him for not phoning; for giving up so easily. Compounding her problems, Julie was sleeping very badly. While her mind might be saying she mustn't see Travis again, her body was giving her a very different message. Her body craved him, unrelentingly.

On Thursday evening, about nine-thirty, the telephone rang. Her mother, Julie thought glumly. No doubt Pearl was wondering why Julie hadn't dropped by all week. She picked up the receiver, trying to inject some energy into her voice. "Hello?"

"It's Travis."

His voice penetrated every pore, filling her with a tumult of helpless desire. She sank down on the nearest chair, clutching the receiver. "I told you to leave me alone," she said, surprised how forceful she sounded.

"I don't always do what I'm told—I thought you knew me well enough by now to realize that. What are your plans for the weekend?"

"I don't have any. With you or anyone else."

"Who else have you gone to bed with since last Sunday?"

"Five different men every night. Six on Tuesday."

"So you don't have time to go out for dinner with me Saturday evening?"

"No, I don't."

"Your loss," Travis said cheerfully, and cut the connection.

Puzzled and vastly disappointed, Julie listened to the hum on the line. He'd given up much too easily; nor had he sounded particularly upset. Nothing like Sunday.

He was getting over her. Already.

This thought should have made her happy. Instead, in a vile mood, she hauled on her Reeboks, went to the park and ran hard for over thirty minutes. Then she went to her fitness club, worked out and lifted weights. Her body was no doubt in better shape after all this activity. But it had done nothing to improve her mood.

She didn't want to be in the same room with Travis ever again. But she didn't want him getting over her too soon. How illogical was that?

Travis got in his car and headed for the clinic, glancing at his watch as he pulled out on the street. Perfect timing. He was being both deceitful and manipulative; but it was all in a good cause. At least, he hoped so.

Julie, as he well knew, had a mind of her own. Maybe she wouldn't even get in the car. Let alone agree to be driven anywhere by him.

It was up to him to persuade her. He'd never been one to back down from a challenge. And Julie was certainly a challenge. He shoved to the back of his mind the thought that he might just be banging his head against a brick wall, that Julie would once again give him the cold shoulder.

That she'd meant it when she'd said she didn't want to see him again.

It couldn't be true. How could he equate that with the woman he'd made love to in her apartment? Her innocence, that told him more clearly than words that her sexual experience had indeed been limited. The bemusement in her face when he'd touched her and she'd been seized by desire. Her generosity, her wholehearted abandonment, her heart-stopping beauty. His hands clenched on the wheel, Travis pulled up at a traffic light. He'd swear on a whole stack of Bibles that he was the first man to bring that woman into existence. So now was he supposed to sit back and allow her to be buried again? All because of her parents?

Or was he simply being an egotistical idiot who couldn't accept the word *no?* Who was acting out of wounded male pride?

He'd left the stately brick buildings of Old Port for the suburbs. The one word he was trying very hard to keep out of his calculations was that awkward word *love.* Bryce had asked him if he was in love with Julie, and he'd denied it instantly. This maelstrom of lust, frustration and longing that had him in its coils had nothing to do with love.

Although how would he know? He wasn't exactly an expert on the subject. And Julie, he suspected, was even less so.

He'd handled finding out she had no plans for the weekend rather well. He only hoped that hadn't changed since last night.

The grounds of the clinic boasted close-clipped lawns and flowerbeds filled with frilly petunias. Travis drove around to the side entrance, the one nearest the physiotherapy department. By some judicious questioning, he'd found out when Julie's shift ended; he'd already known, from conversations he'd had with her, that she took the bus to work, renting a car only when she had an expedition in mind.

He was fifteen minutes early.

It was a very long fifteen minutes, during which he had time to relive every detail of the time he'd spent with Julie, ending with their cataclysmic lovemaking and her obdurate refusal to see him again. For the tenth time, he looked at his watch. She was now five minutes late.

The side door swung open. A dark-haired woman in a crisp white uniform was running down the steps.

Travis got out of the car. Julie saw him instantly and stopped dead on the bottom step. Her face was a study of conflicting emotions; but surely there'd been, elusively, a flash of joy? "Hi, Julie," Travis said. "I was out this way and wondered if you wanted a drive home?"

It wasn't a complete lie. Neither was it the complete truth. "Do you have patients here?" she said suspiciously.

"I come out here sometimes, yes." That at least was the truth, he thought. "Hop in, it'll save you waiting for the bus."

She was chewing on her lower lip; if she had felt joy, it wasn't showing now. "I am tired," she admitted, slowly walking toward his car.

She was standing in the sunlight now; the faint shadows under her eyes filled him with a helpless yearning. "All the more reason to get a lift," Travis said casually as he leaned over and opened the passenger door.

She got in, closed the door and did up her seat belt. His heart thudding against his ribs, Travis said inanely, "Friday afternoons…what would we do without weekends?"

"You said it." She gave him a faint smile. "I thought this job would be a sinecure after some of the overseas stuff I've done. But it's really hard work…although more rewarding than I'd expected."

As he drove out of the grounds, he asked her a few

technical questions, pleased for more than one reason when she launched into a discussion of some controversial new treatments. By the park, instead of turning right, he turned left; only five minutes later did she say, puzzled, "This isn't the way downtown. You're not heading for Old Port... you're going toward the Veterans' Bridge."

His mouth dry, Travis said calmly, "That's right. I'm abducting you."

"*What?*"

"It's summer, you have no plans and neither do I, and there's a wonderful resort on a beach a few miles south of here."

"You're taking me away for the *weekend?*"

"Yep."

"Are you out of your mind?"

"Not that I'm aware of."

"I won't go!"

"Relax, Julie. Live a little."

"Don't you tell me what to do. The next traffic light, I'm out of here."

Travis hadn't rehearsed what he'd do if she reacted this way. "You can do that if you want," he said. "Although if you really don't want to go, I'll drive you home—"

"Oh sure," she interrupted, "you think I believe one word you say?"

"If you're dead set against changing the smallest thing about yourself, I'll drive you straight home," he said in a hard voice. "And that's a promise."

"I did change something! Last Sunday afternoon. I never behave like that, leading a man on, just about hauling him into my bed and then behaving like some kind of sex maniac...I never behave like that. Never!"

He glanced over. Her voice had had a telltale quiver, and tears were filming her eyes. "I know you don't," he said.

"You believe me?"

"Of course I do. For Pete's sake, I was the man you were in bed with. You think I didn't learn a whole lot about you while we were making love?"

"You did?"

"Innocent, trusting, generous, wild…you were all those things. And then you showed me the door faster than you can say *bed*."

She reached into her purse, pulled out a tissue and blew her nose. "That's because you scare the heck out of me."

"You think I'm not scared?" he asked; and with an uncomfortable lurch realized it was true.

She looked full at him. "Come off it, Travis. You, scared?"

"I've never abducted a woman in my life. Never wanted to until you came along. Listen to me for a minute. When I was six, my mother vanished…when I went to bed she was there, and when I woke up in the morning she was gone. I was told she was in New York. But then a few days later, my father told me she'd died. I can't remember a single detail of the funeral, or if any of the relatives came to stay over. When I tried to ask where she was, my father ordered me never to mention her name again. Then he took me to a boarding school outside Boston and left me there. So I lost the island, too, which was a place as near to heaven as I could imagine."

Travis paused. His blue eyes had been very far away; slowly he brought them back to rest on Julie's face. "Something shut down in me after that, and I suppose you could call it love. I don't know what I feel for you, Julie. I only know it's stronger than anything I've ever felt before, and that if I turn my back on it, I'm shortchanging myself and possibly you as well."

He seemed to have run out of words. But he'd just spent two minutes stopped at a red light and she hadn't jumped out of the car.

Julie said blankly, "Well, that was certainly honest."

"Don't ask me why we're pulled to each other the way we are because I don't have the answer," Travis said roughly. "But it's got to mean something. This might sound as conceited as all get-out but I'm going to say it anyway—I think it means something for you, too. Don't run away, Julie. Life's too short for that."

She was gazing down at her clasped hands. "You really were okay with the way I behaved on Sunday?"

"Okay? I loved it…couldn't you tell?"

"I—I guess so."

She didn't sound convinced. He said with all the force of his personality, "You took huge risks, you followed your heart and allowed yourself to be who you really are. That made me feel about ten feet tall—why wouldn't it?"

"Passion," she whispered. "It's such an overused word and I never knew I was capable of it."

"If you spend the weekend with me, neither one of us knows where that'll lead us. But the alternative is to close down. Bury something that's both rare and precious. I don't think we should do that."

She swallowed hard. "Working in Tanzania was a piece of cake compared to this."

"So was Angola," he said wryly.

"I don't have anything to wear except my uniform."

"I bought some stuff for you." He smiled at her. "In the hopes that you were abductable."

"Clothes? For me? How did you know my size?"

"Photographic memory," he said solemnly, and watched her blush. "A couple of dresses, a swimsuit, sandals, underwear and a nightgown."

Her blush deepened. "A nightgown, hmm?"

"There's not much to it."

"I'm frightened, Travis," she muttered.

"I'll do everything in my power to make you happy this

weekend,'' Travis said forcefully. As for what happened after the weekend, he was as ignorant of that as she was. And maybe just as frightened. One day at a time, he told himself and accelerated to the maximum speed.

Half an hour later he'd checked in at the main lodge, and was driving along a narrow dirt road overhung with silver birches toward their chalet. It was the end one, sheltered by thick spruce, with a wide deck facing the beach, where waves danced in the evening sun and rocks gleamed in the wet sand. Julie got out of the car, stretching her legs. "It's a lovely place," she said.

She'd been very quiet for the last part of the journey. He could have asked her about her parents, but something had held him back. Now he said casually, "Why don't we go for dinner, you must be hungry."

The inside of the chalet was luxuriously furnished, the bed king-size, the bathroom fitted with a whirlpool tub. Travis dumped the bag of clothes on the chesterfield that overlooked the ocean. "I hope you like them."

She took out the dresses, her face lighting up with spontaneous pleasure. "They're great—but you must have spent a wad of money."

"We can talk about that later...I'll wait for you on the deck."

He stood by the railing, gazing out to sea, aching to hold her in his arms and reassure himself that she really did want to be here. Don't rush her, Travis, you've got all weekend. And you know perfectly well what'll happen if you touch her.

He went back inside in a few minutes. Julie was just emerging from the bathroom, wearing the sundress he'd picked out because it was as green as her eyes. It also showed rather a lot of bare skin. He said lightly, "Ready to eat?"

She nodded, hurrying for the door. Side by side they

walked back to the lodge. The dining room was on an inlet, overlooking the bay and the sunset's orange and saffron glow. They discussed the menu, the wine list, the weather, his job and hers, meanwhile eating fish chowder and game hens with wild rice. The waiter cleared away their plates, passing them dessert menus. Julie read through hers, chattering away about her addiction for dark chocolate. He'd never thought of her as a woman who had to fill the silence with idle talk.

The waiter left. Travis said with no finesse whatsoever, "I don't want chocolate. I want you."

She dropped the menu and said in a rush, "You haven't as much as touched me since we got here. I thought you'd changed your mind. That you regretted bringing me here."

Nothing could be further from the truth. He reached over and covered her fingers with his, feeling them curl into his palm. "I didn't want to grab you the minute we walked in the door."

"I noticed that."

"I figured I should show a little subtlety this time."

"So is it chocolate mousse or me?" she asked, her dark lashes falling to hide her eyes.

He pushed back his chair, still holding her by the hand. "I'll tell the waiter to put this on our room account...let's go."

"We shouldn't run. It wouldn't look good."

In a voice pitched for her ears alone, he said, "I want you, Julie, don't ever doubt that."

"It's mutual," she said with a dazzling smile that took his breath away.

They didn't actually run to the chalet; but they held hands the whole way, and once they were indoors Travis took Julie in his arms and kissed her with a passionate and protracted intensity that she more than matched. Hastily he detached himself to draw the blinds, watching her kick off her sandals and pull her dress over her head. He'd bought her lace underwear; wondering if his heart could force its way out of his chest, he saw how the sweet curves of her breasts were cupped in the delicate fabric. "Every time I see you," he said huskily, "I can't get over how beautiful you are."

She walked toward him, holding herself proudly under his gaze, the slim lines of her thighs pale in the dusk. "Make love to me, Travis," she said.

He took her by the waist, pulling her toward his hips, where it was more than obvious that he was ready for her. Had he ever known with such certainty that he was exactly where he wanted to be? More than that, he was with the one woman who could fill an inner loneliness he'd scarcely known was his. He pushed this thought aside to examine later, and with all the skill he possessed set out to make Julie as happy to be here as he was.

Later, when Travis looked back on a weekend he knew he'd never forget, there were images that rose in his mind. Julie seducing him in the nightgown he'd bought her, which clung to all her curves and almost bared her breasts. Julie wearing nothing at all, holding out her arms to him in the big bed. The play of expression on her face. The soft, intimate sound of her breathing in the middle of the night, as she slept curled into his body. Her laughter. Her grace. Her sudden tears after a lovemaking as elemental as a cyclone...

They made it to the dining room for Saturday lunch and Sunday breakfast. Once, they walked on the beach for fifteen minutes. The rest of the time they spent in the chalet, ordering room service when they realized they were hungry for something other than each other. They talked very little, letting their bodies speak for them. If Travis thought about it at all, he must have decided subliminally to leave the subject of Julie's parents for another time. He and Julie were building a foundation for the future; any discussions would be better based on that foundation.

He had no idea what he meant by that vague word *future*.

On Sunday morning after they'd made love in the tub, splashing rather a lot of water on the floor in the process, he said, "I wish we could stay all week...I'm not ready to go home."

She gave a lazy chuckle. "I'm going back to work to rest up."

"Can't take the pace, huh?"

"You're too much for me."

"Haven't heard you complaining."

She swiped at his chest with the towel, her smile fading. "This has been a perfect weekend, Travis. But we do have to go back to normal."

He captured her hand in his. "I've got meetings tomorrow night that I can't get out of. But why don't you come to my place on Tuesday after work?"

She brought their linked hands to her cheek, closing her eyes. "I can't get enough of you," she said faintly.

"I'm not going to vanish the minute we leave here, Julie."

So he'd understood, she thought slowly. "This has been so magical, how can we possibly transpose it to our ordinary lives?" she said with a touch of desperation.

"We can. And we will."

The dark hair on his chest was sleek as a seal's pelt. She laid her other palm over his heart, feeling its steady pounding against her skin. "Tuesday night," she said with attempted levity. "It's a date. And now I guess I'd better get some clothes on. I'll wear the other dress, the one I haven't tried yet."

"It's the color of the ocean where I first saw you," Travis said.

Her lashes flickered. Once again, in a few words, he'd

pierced her to the heart. She walked back into the bedroom, pulled on her underwear and slipped the dress over her head. Then she stood still, trying to memorize her surroundings. A sun-drenched room with the sound of waves and the soft whisper of pine boughs coming through the open windows. And a bed in which she'd found a happiness she hadn't known existed.

How was she going to bear leaving here?

She wanted to stay forever.

CHAPTER TWELVE

BY MONDAY evening, Julie wasn't sure about anything. In the middle of the night, she'd woken up in her three-quarter bed reaching for Travis; he hadn't, of course, been there. But rather than waking to memories of the bliss she'd experienced in his arms, she'd instantly been suffused by a cold anxiety that she couldn't dispel, no matter how many parakeets she counted.

Yes, it had been a fabulous weekend. The ultimate getaway with a handsome, sexy man. But one weekend didn't make a relationship; had nothing to do with permanence. While she was almost sure Travis wanted to keep on seeing her, what did she want?

She didn't want commitment. She certainly didn't want marriage. So why was she even contemplating seeing him again? Wasn't she getting deeper into trouble every time they got together?

Or did she just want a series of wild weekends that were utterly divorced from her normal life? Even she could see that wouldn't work, not with a man like Travis.

Eventually Julie went back to sleep, the alarm waking her from dreams that left her feeling frazzled and exhausted. She worked all day, caught the bus home and had leftovers for supper. The apartment seemed very empty without Travis and tomorrow evening an age away.

But she didn't want intimacy. She didn't.

Even if she scarcely knew what it was.

With an impatient sigh Julie changed her clothes and went out for a walk. She crossed the cobblestone street, her brow furrowed in thought. Travis had suggested she sleep at his place last night; but she'd demurred. He was moving too quickly for her, she needed time alone, one by one she'd trotted out all the clichés. She believed every one of them. So why did she miss him so unceasingly?

Then her steps slowed. Consciously or unconsciously, she'd been walking in the direction of her parents' street. She might as well drop in. Considering everything that had happened to her since last Friday, she might even see them with new eyes.

It was worth a try. But when she climbed the front steps of the freshly painted bungalow and rang the doorbell, there was no answer; her father's car was gone from the driveway. They'd probably be back soon. She'd been wanting to go through some of her old books in the attic in order to reread a couple of them; now was as good a time as any. She let herself in with the key her mother had given her, and went straight upstairs. The attic was very warm, and rather less tidy than the rest of Pearl's domain.

Which box had the books been stored in? And why hadn't she labeled it? Julie started opening boxes at random, finding sets of old dishes, all her father's account books for the last twenty years, and then a box of old photo albums. She picked up the first album, suddenly curious. Below it, facedown, was a gold-framed photograph. Carefully Julie lifted it out and turned it over.

It was a wedding photo of a young couple, the bride in a slim-fitting white dress with a trailing bouquet of roses, the groom lean and handsome in a tuxedo. The bride's arm was tucked confidingly into her new husband's, his hand lying protectively over hers; they were both smiling radiantly into the camera.

It took Julie a full ten seconds to realize that the two people in the photograph were her parents. The groom was Thomas, the bride Pearl.

She sat back on her heels, staring at the two faces with

strained intensity. They looked so carefree, so joyful. More than that, she realized, as all her new knowledge came to the fore, they looked physically close, their body language speaking of the bed they would share that night.

They were total strangers to her. Had she ever seen them look like that in real life?

No. Never.

Happiness doesn't last, she thought numbly. Neither does desire. Thomas and Pearl had once been as delighted with each other's company as she and Travis had been all weekend. While it might be true that not all relationships head the same way, it could equally be true that she and Travis could be as doomed as her parents, and the thought made Julie go cold.

She grabbed for the next picture frame, her hands shaking so badly she almost dropped it. Her mother and father in a formal pose, Pearl holding a three-year-old in a pretty pink dress. The child was herself. Thomas was standing stiffly behind his seated wife, his hand placed on her shoulder with a rigid correctness; while both he and Pearl were smiling, the radiance was gone. These were smiles for the camera, not smiles of spontaneous happiness.

Something had gone wrong by the time she was three. Had it been her fault? Hadn't they wanted her?

With a whimper of distress Julie put the photos back in the box, jammed the album on top of them and closed the cardboard flaps. Her books were forgotten. She scrambled to her feet, wiping the dust from her shorts, and ran downstairs. The driveway was still empty. In such a confused state of mind that she was frantic to be gone before her parents returned, she quickly locked the door behind her and hurried down the street.

There was no sign of her father's car. Nor, when she got back to her apartment building, was it parked near there; now ironic if they'd been trying to visit her while she was at their place. She scurried upstairs. Never had her apartment seemed such a haven. Throwing herself down on the chesterfield, Julie realized that she was crying. They were slow tears of despair, loss and deep sadness, all the anxieties she'd locked away since childhood pouring out.

She was crying for her parents, for the happiness and intimacy that they'd lost. She was also crying for herself. For, of course, this confirmed all her fears. Any long-term relationship with Travis was out of the question. She couldn't bear to experience the slow erosion of passion, or the destruction of the intimacy she'd so tentatively explored in his embrace.

It was all too easily lost, leaving nothing but emptiness and bitter memories.

Nothing was to be trusted, happiness least of all.

She mustn't see Travis again.

Julie took this resolve to bed with her, cried herself to sleep, and woke heavy-eyed in the morning. She was busy all day at the clinic, and glad to be so; when she got home, there was a message on her machine from Travis. "Call me as soon as you get in. I'll take you out for dinner—the contents of my refrigerator look like a bacteriology experiment gone wrong. But I did change the sheets on the bed. See you soon."

She mustn't cry. Not again.

She'd better phone him. Get it over with.

All her movements leaden, she picked up the receiver and punched in his number. He picked it up on the first ring. "Julie?"

He sounded so eager. So happy, she thought with a pang of pure agony. Her voice seemed to have disappeared. "Julie," he repeated sharply, "are you there?"

"Yes," she croaked.

"What's the matter? You sound terrible."

What was worse, his happiness or his concern, so immediate she could almost feel it? "I—Travis, I'm not coming over tonight. Or any night. We mustn't see each other again."

"*What* did you say?"

"I don't want to see you again," she said more strongly.

"Stay where you are. I'm coming over."

"No, you can't!" But he was gone. Slowly she put the receiver back in its cradle.

She was still in her uniform. But what did it matter? She'd repeat what she'd already told him and then he'd really be gone. Forever, this time. The way it had to be.

She went to the bathroom and washed her face in cold water, carefully applying blusher and lipstick in an effort to make herself presentable. All too soon, the buzzer rang, loudly and imperatively. A cold lump of dread lodged somewhere below her heart, Julie went to the door.

Travis walked in, closed the door and took her in his arms. For a moment she sagged against him, oblivious to everything but the comfort and security of his embrace, the familiar warmth of his body. Then she stiffened, pushing him away. He stared down at her, missing, she was sure, not one detail of her ravaged appearance. "What's up?"

She said rapidly, "I can't go on with this. I don't want to see you again."

"You already told me that. Why, Julie? What's happened between Sunday afternoon and now?"

"Passion, happiness, love—none of them last."

"They last if you want them to. If you work at it."

"You might believe that. I don't."

His eyes narrowed. "You weren't talking this way on Sunday. Have you seen your parents since then?"

"Why can't you just accept what I'm saying?"

"Because it's not good enough. We're lovers, we spent the weekend together—and now you think you can fob me off with a bunch of generalizations about happiness?"

"All right, then. Let me tell you what happened." Speaking very fast, she described what she'd found in the attic and how it had affected her. "My parents were happy once. Just like us on the weekend. You've never met them…but believe me, they're not happy now." Her voice broke. "They hate each other. But they're too damn polite to say so. So they snipe at each other continually, until I can't bear to be around them. It was like that the whole time I was growing up, a thin layer of civility that hid any honest emotions, so that I never knew what was really going on. What I could trust."

She was crying again. She swiped at her cheeks, furious with herself. "There were all kinds of petty rules that I was supposed to obey. All for my own good, of course. Especially once I reached puberty, because heaven forbid there should be any straight talk about sex. I don't know if they even had any sex. They never touched each other and I can't remember my father ever giving my mother a hug."

She jammed her hands in the pockets of her uniform. "I rebelled against almost all the rules and left home the summer I graduated from high school." Scowling at him, she went on, "The one area where I didn't rebel was sex. I was afraid to, I guess. I think even then I sensed I'd be in real trouble if I did. And I was right. This weekend proves my point. I'm not going to end up like my parents, I'd rather be single my whole life. So I want you to go now. And I don't want to see you again."

He took her by the shoulders. "We wouldn't end up like your parents—I know we wouldn't."

She could feel the force of his willpower, unbending as steel, and called on all her reserves to withstand it. "I disagree."

"This is the second time you've pulled this stunt—made love with me, then shown me the door."

"I can't help it! Don't you see, Travis? Now is the time to end this, while it's still just sex between us, while we—"

"Just sex?" he interrupted incredulously. "Is that all I mean to you?"

"We spent the whole weekend in bed. What's that if it's not sex?"

"We made love, Julie."

"That's just an expression. A cover-up—like my parents' politeness. We had sex, Travis. Great sex. Amazing sex. But don't let's pretend it was anything else."

"If that's what you think," he said in a hard voice, "then I'm out of here. I won't be treated as a prize stud. Not by you or anyone else."

Inadvertently she'd found the weapon she needed. "I don't see what the big deal is," she said coldly. "Sex like we had is probably pretty rare. But it's still just sex."

"I wasn't even a person to you, was I?" he said with icy control. "And I thought it was supposed to be men who were guilty of that particular fault."

She wanted to cry out that he was wrong, that it had been something about him, specific and impelling, that had broken through her self-imposed celibacy. But she couldn't tell him. She had to end this quickly, before she broke down and wept like a baby. "Don't try to tell me you're in love with me," she said, "because I won't believe it."

"Whether I am or not is none of your business," he grated. "It's been a long time since I misread someone so badly...you'd think I'd know better by now. Goodbye, Julie. Have a nice life."

Very quietly he shut the door behind him. Moving like an old woman, Julie snapped the latch and put the chain in its slot. Then she walked into her bedroom, threw herself across the quilt and began to weep.

Three weeks went by, during which Julie went through the motions at home and at work. The days at work were the least difficult, because she enjoyed her patients and was enough of a professional to shut out her personal life. The nights alone in her spindle bed were the worst. There, Travis haunted her waking thoughts and her dreams; after ten days she had blue shadows under her eyes and had lost four pounds.

On the weekends she went camping in the Adirondacks, had dinner with Kathy and Michael, and attended a three-day music festival; any activity was preferable to sitting in her apartment staring at the four walls and remembering with aching clarity the passion-filled hours she'd spent with Travis at the resort. As the days—and nights—slowly passed, he made no attempt to get in touch with her. And how could she blame him?

It was always a relief to go back to work on Monday mornings. The Monday after the festival was particularly busy. At two-thirty, Julie grabbed a coffee and a muffin and went to the empty staff room with them. The muffin was stuffed with fruit and bran; she chewed it valiantly, wishing her appetite would come back. To top it off, she felt bone-tired from morning to night. It really had been just sex between her and Travis, she thought fiercely, washing down the muffin with a gulp of coffee. Sex, plain and simple.

"You look very militant, Julie," an amused voice said from the doorway.

With a nervous start, Julie looked up. Then she put down the last of the muffin and smiled with genuine pleasure. "Leonora," she said, "how nice to see you. But have I missed something? Do you have an appointment today?"

Leonora Connolly had had a series of appointments with Julie earlier in the summer. She was a tall, statuesque woman with very blue eyes, and a wealth of dark hair faintly streaked with grey. Julie had liked her from the start, and had done her best to alleviate some of the damage that a lifetime as a professional dancer had inflicted on Leonora's tendons and ligaments.

Leonora smiled. "May I come in? No, I don't have an appointment. I was visiting a friend who's been admitted here for a few days, and thought I'd drop by and tell you how much better I've been feeling since our sessions. I'm so grateful to you."

"Don't forget that you worked hard, too," Julie laughed. "I can't claim all the credit. Can I get you a coffee? As hospital coffee goes, it's not bad."

"No, thanks, I can't stay."

Julie's brow furrowed in puzzlement. "You know, it's funny but you remind me of someone. Someone I've seen recently…"

"Oh?" Leonora said, her jaw tensing slightly.

Her fingers unconsciously tightening around her cup, Julie said flatly, "Oh. I remember now. It doesn't matter."

"Tell me who, Julie. Please."

There was an insistence in Leonora's voice that took Julie by surprise. With huge reluctance she said, "I met a Dr. Travis Strathern a few weeks ago. His eyes are very like yours, such a deep blue…Leonora, what's wrong?"

For the other woman had paled, briefly looking every year of her age. Leaning against the doorframe, she blurted, "Did you like him?"

"He's apparently a very fine doctor," Julie said evasively.

"I didn't mean professionally. As a man. What did you think of him?"

Gossip and indiscretion were characteristics Julie would never have applied to Leonora Connolly. Puzzlement overcoming her reluctance, Julie said, "Travis? Forceful, charismatic, articulate. He says it like it is. No games." She grimaced. "Tall, dark and handsome. A male counterpart to you, in that respect."

Leonora said faintly, "I see."

"Do you know him? Leonora, you don't look well, can I get you something?"

"He's my son," Leonora said.

Her head whirling, Julie put her cup down on the table. Whatever she might have expected Leonora to say, it wouldn't have been this.

For Travis's mother was dead.

CHAPTER THIRTEEN

THE silence stretched out. Realizing she had to say something, Julie faltered, "Leonora, Travis can't be your son. He told me his mother died when he was six."

"It's a long story," Leonora said. Awkwardly she straightened, looking every year of her age. "Is there somewhere we could go to talk in private?"

The grace and elegance of Leonora's movements had been the first thing Julie had noticed about her; although this soon had been followed by admiration for her innate dignity of spirit. For Leonora to abandon both must mean that she was deeply upset. "We could go to my office," Julie said. "It's small, but I can close the door."

Quickly she led the way down the corridor, ushering Leonora into a cubicle that contained little more than a desk, two chairs and some shelves. She closed the door and sat down. "I shouldn't have mentioned the likeness between you and Travis," she said remorsefully. "I didn't mean to upset you."

"How well do you know him?"

And how was she supposed to answer that? "I met him at a party. I've only seen him a couple of times since then," Julie said, more or less truthfully.

"I have to tell someone what this is all about," Leonora said helplessly. "It's driving me mad."

"Take your time," Julie said gently.

"Yes." Leonora took a deep breath and launched herself. "I always wanted to be a dancer. I started lessons when I was just a child, and it was obvious from the beginning that I had more than ordinary talent. And then when

I was eighteen, I met a man called Charles Strathern. Handsome, forceful, dynamic…well, you get the picture. I fell madly in love and into his bed without once considering the consequences. It's an old story, Julie. I ended up at the altar pregnant. Travis was born five months later.''

Julie sat very still, her heart racing under her uniform. Instinctively she knew Leonora was telling the truth; nor was it difficult to picture this imperious, talented woman as Travis's mother. "Go on," she said softly.

"I tried my best to be a good mother. But in essence I don't have a maternal bone in my body. I soon went back to dancing lessons, and then began teaching dance in Boston, getting away from all my responsibilities as often as I could. It wasn't enough, because the whole artistic scene on the East Coast was too conservative for my taste; but I had to make do with what was available. I'd realized a year after I was married that Charles wasn't the man for me, but I made the best of that, too. Then, when Travis was five, I got pregnant again, this time with twins.''

"Twins?" Julie echoed.

"A boy and a girl, born just after Travis turned six. Brent and Jenessa.'' Leonora looked down at her fingers, clenched in her lap. "I felt so trapped, so confined. At first I was angry with the whole world. But I couldn't take that anger out on my children, it wasn't their fault. So it turned inward, and I grew more and more depressed. Finally, I went to New York, to see a world-renowned psychiatrist whom Charles knew…there was a recital while I was there by an avant garde dancer from Paris, Madeleine Mercier. I went to see her dance, and two days later I, too, was in Paris. I simply ran away. Abandoned my marriage and ~y children.''

Her head buzzing with questions, Julie sat very still. There was more to come, she knew.

"I'd never been known for forethought,'' Leonora said

wryly. "The day I arrived in Paris, I phoned Charles, to tell him I'd fly home every two months to see the children. He said I was to change my name, and that if I ever showed my face in Boston or on Manatuck again, he'd ruin me. His lawyers, he said, would be sending me divorce papers, and he would get sole custody of the children." She gave a reminiscent shudder. "I thought of flying home that very day. But Madeleine had already taken me on as a pupil, and I was sure if I waited a few weeks he'd calm down. However, by the time I got in touch with him again, he'd already told Travis that I had died. I found out later he'd invented a fictitious funeral in Philadelphia, where I was born. The twins, of course, were too young to know about any of this."

"How could Charles have done that to his own son?" Julie said, aghast.

"I'd wounded his pride. I'd made a fool of him."

"He's never told Travis the truth about you."

"That's why I'm here. To make peace with Travis, if that's possible. But I've been too afraid to contact him." She gave Julie a shaky smile. "It's ludicrous, isn't it? I'm living in the same town, and I haven't made a move to see him. Or the twins. Brent, I gather, works in Boston, while Jenessa's an artist, living in a little village west of Boston."

Travis had never once mentioned that he had a sister. Nor, for that matter, had Brent. Julie said reluctantly, "After you left, Travis was sent away to boarding school, and for two years wasn't even allowed back to Manatuck."

"One more betrayal...he loved that place." Leonora raised her head, with its crown of dark hair. "Julie, I'm going to ask a favor of you. A huge favor. You've met Travis. He trusts you enough that he's told you what happened when he was six. I want you to tell him that I didn't die, that I'm here in Portland, and I want to see him. You could prepare him, so that it won't be such a terrible shock for him."

"I couldn't!"

"Please…I don't often beg for anything, I have more than my share of pride, too. But I'm begging you now. The truth is, I'm afraid. Afraid that he won't consent to see me at all." Her smile was twisted. "I've danced in front of the toughest critics in Europe, and I'm afraid of my own son. But why should Travis want to see me? I left him, abandoned him, ran away as though he didn't matter at all."

Leonora's eyes were bleak with remembered sorrow. Briefly Julie rested her head in her hands. "I don't really know Travis that well," she said in a muffled voice.

"Let me tell you something—I liked you from the first moment I met you. You're honest and courageous. You, more than anyone I know, can do this."

For a wild moment Julie considered telling Leonora about the weekend she'd spent in Travis's arms; and how she'd then sent him away, because she, too, was afraid of him. She looked up. "I'll do it," she said, her voice sounding as though it came from a long way away. "But you've got to give me a couple of days to think about it, and rehearse what I'm going to say."

"Of course." Leonora slowly unclenched her hands. "Thank you, Julie. More than I can say."

"Maybe we should wait to see how this all turns out before you thank me."

"You'll do the best you can. The rest is up to Travis."

Julie pushed herself to her feet. Her cold hands pressing against the desk, she said, "I've got to go back to work, Leonora. I have an appointment in five minutes."

The older woman hesitated. "You'll let me know as soon as you see Travis?"

"Yes, of course," Julie replied. Briefly Leonora rested

one hand on Julie's shoulder; then she walked away down the empty corridor.

Julie watched her go. Three weeks ago she'd told Travis their relationship was over. Now she was committed to seeking him out, as the bearer of shattering news.

To say that she was afraid was a massive understatement. And yet, beneath the terror, wasn't there a grain of pure joy that she would be seeing him again?

Travis was late home from work on Wednesday evening. It had been an exhausting day. Far too much paperwork, two patients who seemed to think he had nothing to do but immerse himself in their imaginary symptoms, and a tragic prognosis he'd had to deliver to another of his patients, a young woman with three small children.

His exhaustion stemmed from more than a bad day at work. Try as he might, he couldn't get Julie out of his system. More times than he'd care to admit he'd pulled back with his hand actually on the receiver to phone her; twice he'd driven past her apartment, just to see the lights glowing from her narrow windows. He was obsessed with her, he thought savagely. Worse, nothing he did loosened her grip one iota.

He hated being so helpless. So entrapped.

He tossed a package of frozen pasta in the microwave and hit the buttons. He didn't even like pasta. But he lacked the energy to barbecue anything, and he didn't want to eat by himself in a restaurant.

He was a mess.

He went into the bedroom, hauling his shirt over his head and searching for a clean T-shirt in the drawer. He should do a wash. Maybe he'd get around to it on the weekend. Although Bryce, on their last conversation, had suggested that Travis make use of Bryce's cottage north of Portland next weekend. Get the hell out of that condo, is what Bryce had actually said. Along with a fair number of uncomplimentary remarks about Julie.

What was he going to do at the cottage? Think about Julie from Friday night to Sunday evening, that's what.

The T-shirt slung over one shoulder, Travis went back into the kitchen and opened the microwave. He'd forgotten to pry open the corner of the pasta box. Steam had ruptured the cardboard seal, splattering rigatoni all over one wall of the microwave. Then the doorbell rang, a melodious chiming that made Travis swear out loud. If it was the blond bombshell down the hallway who was pursuing him with all the subtlety of a bulldozer, she was right out of luck.

Not bothering to look through the peephole, he yanked the door open, a blistering refusal already on his tongue. His jaw dropped. *"Julie!"* he gasped.

In one quick glance he took in every detail of her appearance: slim white jeans, a coral silk shirt with the sleeves rolled up, coral lipstick and blusher and eyes a wide, terrified green. She'd come back, he thought in a great flood of gratitude and joy. She'd changed her mind.

He put his arms around her waist, lifted her over the threshold, slammed the door shut with one foot and began kissing her. He could feel the shock run through her, the sudden rigidity of her spine, and ignored both. She'd come back. She was in his arms, where she belonged. His Julie, his beautiful Julie…

With another of those surges of passionate gratitude, he realized she was kissing him back, her hips pressed to his, her palms clasping his bare ribcage. Her lips were soft and warm, she smelled delicious, her body fitted his embrace as though made for it. He forgot what a desert the last three weeks had been, forgot that he was furious with her for leaving him. Swinging her off her feet, he headed for the bedroom.

The bed wasn't made and there was dirty laundry scattered all over the rug. But what did that matter?

Wholly intent on where he was going, it took Travis several seconds to realize Julie was beating on his chest with her fists. "Travis, let me down!"

He smiled at her, a smile of unquenchable happiness. "Hey, stop that. You came here to make love with me and I'd rather do that in bed than on the hall floor."

"I didn't!"

"Sure you did. You don't kiss a platonic friend the way you were just kissing me."

"Travis, I didn't come here to go to bed with you," she said frantically. "I have something to tell you, something very important."

He looked at her blankly for the space of five full seconds. "You're pregnant."

"I'm not! Don't be silly."

"There's nothing silly about it. That rainy Sunday afternoon at your place we made love twice, and neither time did we use protection. That, dear Julie, is how babies get made."

"This is something else altogether," she said impatiently. "I don't even know where to begin but I sure know it isn't in your bedroom." Still pushing at his chest, she looked around her. "Which is a mess."

He put her down, his hands tight on her shoulders. She meant it. She hadn't come here to revive their affair. "So what if my bedroom's like a pigsty?" he snarled. "I miss you day and night and doing the laundry hasn't been a priority."

"I didn't mean to kiss you back," she quavered, "I'm sorry about that. It just…happened."

"Oh sure. You had nothing to do with it."

She wriggled her shoulders free. "I'm going into the

living room, you're going to pour me a glass of wine and then you're going to shut up and listen to me!''

"It had better be good, that's all I can say."

He followed her down the hall, trying to ignore the swing of her hips in her white pants. "Find a chair," he said. "White wine or red?"

"Red. The more robust the better."

He opened a very expensive bottle of Merlot and poured two glasses. Julie was standing by the window, looking out over the harbor. When he passed her the glass, she took a gulp and said raggedly, "Earlier this week, I found out something about your past. Now I've come to tell you about it. It's big stuff, Travis, so please listen carefully…I'll do my best to give it to you straight."

For the first time since she'd arrived, Travis really heard her. His nerves tightened. What did she mean? What could she have found out about him to make her look so serious? He, too, took a substantial mouthful of wine.

She began with Leonora, whose eyes so strikingly resembled Travis's, and slowly unfolded that long-ago story of abandonment and deceit. Travis had been sitting on one arm of a leather-covered chair; when she got to the fake funeral in Philadelphia, he stood up. Taking her by the arm, he said harshly, "You're not making this up?"

"You know I wouldn't do that."

He raked his fingers through his hair. "So this is true, what you're telling me."

"Yes."

His ears were ringing, while his head felt as though it were floating somewhere above his body. His mother was alive. That was what Julie was telling him. She was now describing Leonora's long career in Europe, and her recent return to the States, each word inscribing itself indelibly on his brain. Was he going to wake up, and find out he'd been dreaming?

"Because I'd told her I'd met you, Leonora asked me to come and see you," Julie finished. "To break the news to you. She's an exceptional woman, Travis, I've liked her from the first moment we met. So I agreed."

She couldn't think of anything else to say. Travis looked stunned, as though she'd hit him on the head with a two-by-four. And why wouldn't he? His father had told him his mother had died; and that lie had stood unchallenged since Travis had been a little boy. She waited to see what he would do, her one longing to put her arms around him and offer him comfort.

She couldn't do that. Because she'd end up in his bed.

Quickly she pulled a folded piece of paper from her pocket and passed it to him. "This is Leonora's phone number and address. She's hoping you'll get in touch with her. I said I'd ask your permission to give her your phone number."

Travis looked at her as if she were a creature from an alien planet. "I'm supposed to get in touch with her?"

"Or else she'll phone you," Julie said patiently.

"She's expecting me to pick up where we left off twenty-eight years ago?"

"Of course not. But she very much wants to see you."

He said in a hard voice, "I'll think about it."

"I can see it's been a terrible shock—"

"She didn't die. She walked out on me and the twins. You think that makes me want to see her?"

"Don't shoot the messenger, Travis," Julie said softly.

He let out his breath in a long sigh. "Yeah...if I go and see her, you're coming with me."

"Me? This has nothing to do with me!"

"You know her. She thought enough of you to make you the go-between."

Julie swallowed. She was being drawn in deeper and deeper. Yet wouldn't Leonora also welcome her presence?

Leonora, she knew, was terrified of seeing Travis again
And maybe she herself could help in some way to smooth
the path of a meeting fraught with pitfalls. She took a deep
breath. "All right," she said steadily, "I'll go. When?"

"I didn't think you'd agree quite so easily," he said, an
ugly edge to his voice. "This Leonora must be quite the
woman."

"Worthy to be your mother," Julie said evenly.

"Friday evening. Seven-thirty. I'll pick you up at your
apartment."

"Travis, I'm sure she regrets—"

"Will you go to bed with me?"

Julie flinched. "No."

"Then finish your wine and get out of here. I'm not in
the mood for chitchat."

It would be all too easy to make a scathing retort. Julie
put her glass down. "This must have been a terrible
shock."

"Keep your sympathy—I don't need it."

She raised her chin. "I'll see you on Friday."

"I'll look forward to it," he said with heavy sarcasm.

Julie stalked to the door of the condo and let herself out
It shut behind her with a decisive snap. She went home
phoned Leonora to let her know about Friday, evaded any
discussion of Travis's reaction, then went for a run at the
park. It was only when a mallard waddled in front of her
followed by two fluffy brown and yellow ducklings, that
she remembered something.

Travis had thought she was pregnant.

She wasn't. Of course. Although he was right: When the
two of them had fallen into her bed, they'd used no pro
tection.

In the heat of the moment, it had never occurred to her
which showed how out of practice she was, she thought
ruefully. And she was willing to bet it wasn't Travis's usua

style. Her brow furrowed. Her period was notoriously ir-regular; for years she'd blamed this on a combination of tropical heat and antimalarial pills. But as she counted backward in her mind, her steps slowed. She'd never been this late before.

Coincidence, she thought brusquely. And hadn't she read somewhere that stress could foul up your cycle? She'd had enough emotional ups and downs since she'd met Travis to skew any woman's cycle. She wasn't pregnant. Just the same, she wasn't going to tempt fate by going to bed with Travis again.

Then another, equally unpleasant thought occurred to her. Leonora had fallen head over heels in love with Charles; but seven years later had run away from him, from their children and their marriage. One more example of a love that had died, and one more reason she was right to keep her distance from a man with eyes so blue that they saw right through her.

CHAPTER FOURTEEN

FRIDAY evening found Julie sorting through her wardrobe. Jeans wouldn't cut it for this crucial meeting of mother and son. Nor was she going to wear either of the dresses Travis had given her. Frowning, she chose a softly swirling skirt and sleeveless top in malachite-green, with matching sandals she'd bought from a vendor in Athens. She was waiting downstairs in the lobby when Travis drew up in his black car. She ran outdoors and climbed in the passenger seat. Busying herself with the seat belt, she said, "How was your day?"

He said tightly, "Every time I see you, it's as though I've never seen you before...there's this jolt in my chest just like I'd stuck my finger in an electric socket."

"The whole reason I didn't look at you when I got in was to avoid just that reaction," she said irritably. "So what, Travis? We aren't going to act on it, that's the point."

"The gospel according to St. Julie."

"That's unworthy of you!"

"I'm not in the mood to fight fair."

"At least give Leonora a fair hearing," she flashed.

He pulled away from the curb without answering. She sneaked a glance at his profile, which was unyielding, hard-jawed and tight-lipped. He was impeccably dressed in tailored trousers, blue shirt and a silk tie. Just like we were going on a date, she thought painfully.

Nothing could be further from the truth.

Ten minutes later Travis was following Julie up the steps of an attractive apartment complex only five minutes from the clinic. Give Leonora a fair hearing, Julie had said t him. As though that was a simple choice. They rode up in the elevator, then he was striding down a gold-carpeted hallway behind her. Julie tapped on one of the varnished doors, walked in and gestured for him to enter. Feeling like a robot whose circuits had shorted, Travis stepped inside.

The woman who had been waiting for them said with poignant restraint, "Hello, Travis."

She was tall, elegant and instantly remembered. Older, obviously, but in an essential way unchanged. He felt as though he were a little boy again; he also felt an upsurge of purely adult rage that he did his best to tamp down. Shaking hands with her would be absurd; yet he wasn't ready to hug her. He said stiffly, "I asked Julie to be here, I hope you don't mind."

"Not at all." Leonora produced the semblance of a smile. "Julie's been a good friend to me…can I get you a drink?"

A few minutes later Travis found himself seated by a bay window across from his mother. His mother. He said ironically, raising his glass, "Cheers…Julie told me you had a very successful career in Europe. It's funny I never read about you."

"One of your father's conditions was that I change my name…Connolly was my grandmother's maiden name. Added to that, such success as I had was in a fairly narrow field. Avant garde dance isn't to everyone's taste."

The evening light struck her high cheekbones, so like his own. Although she looked poised, her speech had been stilted, and a little muscle was jumping in her jaw. "You've taken a long time to get in touch," he said.

"Your father made me promise never to get in touch with you…I've kept that promise for nearly thirty years. But there's nothing he can do to harm me now. So I came back." She suddenly leaned forward. "You have every right to be angry with me, Travis, don't think I don't understand that.''

"The twins never even knew you."

"Nor I them."

"That was your choice."

"I was never a maternal woman. The mistake I made was in marrying Charles."

"So you admit you made mistakes."

"Have you never done something you've bitterly regretted?"

He leaned forward, feeling his shirt pull tight against his shoulder blades. "I've never married or had children—that way I can't abandon my wife or my child. That's one mistake I won't make."

"I had no idea Charles would react so cruelly! I was young, on my own in Paris, threatened with ruin if I as much as wrote you a letter. Charles wielded a lot of influence—even from Boston he could have made my life untenable."

"Just the same, I'm sure you understand my difficulty," Travis said. "You couldn't be faulted for dying. Very few of us want to do that. But for abandoning me to my father's less than tender mercies—yes, I fault you for that. If you were young, I was much younger. Just a boy. And very much alone."

Tears were glittering in Leonora's blue eyes. Julie saw them and forced herself to keep quiet. This scene was between mother and son; now that she'd brought the players together, she had no lines to speak. She only wished she could rid herself of that recurrent image of a motherless dark-haired boy exiled from his beloved island, set down among strangers in a distant school. No wonder he'd never trusted enough to marry or have children.

"When I left for Paris, I had every intention of returning to Boston five or six times a year," Leonora said. "Wha happened to you was terrible, far beyond anything I could have contemplated. But now I'm asking you as an adult to try to forgive me for my part in that. What your father did is between you and him."

"Unfortunately Charles was no more a paternal figure than you were maternal. Jenessa never goes near him. Nor, since I was sixteen, have I. Brent is the heir apparent."

"I plan to get in touch with both of them," Leonora said flatly. "But it was essential that I approach you first."

"If you're expecting gratitude, you're out of luck."

"Just give me a chance, Travis, that's all I ask."

Travis tossed back his drink. "If you want to tell me about your career, I'll listen."

As a concession, it was a small one, Julie thought, trying to see it as better than nothing. The conversation limped along. Julie sipped her white wine and when Travis stood up twenty minutes later, was heartily glad to get to her feet.

Goodbyes were said. Briefly, a further meeting was discussed, without any decision being reached as to time or place. Travis made no move to touch his mother, nor did Leonora reach out for him. Then Julie and Travis were retracing their steps to his vehicle. Her jaws aching with tension, Julie sat in silence as he drove back to Old Port. He pulled up outside her apartment. "Thank you for coming with me," he said.

He sounded cold and distant rather than grateful. She said evenly, "I can't very well start a fight with you when we're parked on the sidewalk outside my apartment. Too bad."

"You want a fight, Julie?"

"Yes, as a matter of fact, I do."

"I'd be delighted to oblige."

"Then let's go in."

She wasn't inviting him in for any reason other than to blow off steam, thought Julie. Sex was the last thing on her mind. They climbed the steps in a taut silence. As soon as she'd closed the door of her apartment, she went on the offensive. "You've had since Wednesday to absorb the facts, Travis—your mother's alive and well and living in Portland. What are you going to do about her?"

"My mother died a long time ago."

"You've been given what a lot of people would give a fortune for—a second chance."

"Then I'm not most people."

"You can't just ignore her!"

"Try me."

"That's horribly cruel."

"I grieved her loss for years and now all of sudden she reappears and asks for my forgiveness," he said with brutal clarity. "Yet you think I should instantly forget the past and start acting like a son again? Give me a break. Life doesn't work like that."

"There's something else—why did you never mention to me that you had a sister? That Brent had a twin? Are there any other little surprises you've been keeping from me? Stray wives I'm likely to meet on the street? Children scattered around the globe?"

"No—I don't operate that way! Jenessa never comes within ten miles of Dad, and there was enough going on that weekend on Manatuck that I just plain didn't get around to mentioning her."

Rather grudgingly, Julie found she could accept this. But she wasn't finished. "You know how I see it? You're so lucky to have a mother like Leonora. She's artistic and talented and passionate. She takes risks. She's out of the ordinary."

"That's the problem—don't you see?" he retorted. "A six-year-old wants an ordinary mother. One who's there at bedtime and in the morning when he gets up. One he can take his problems to as well as his accomplishments. Sure

Leonora's had an amazing career. But from my perspective, the cost was too high.''

Her eyes blazing, Julie demanded, ''Would you have preferred a mother like mine, who was always there and never stopped trying to control me? Who was so scared of her emotions she buried them all, and denied me my own along with it? My mother's no more maternal than Leonora—Leonora's just more honest about it. And I'm like you, I've never married, either. Too scared to. Too afraid that I might turn out like my mother.''

To her horror Julie suddenly collapsed on the chesterfield, buried her face in her hands and started to cry. Travis sat down beside her, clumsily putting his arms around her. She struck him away. ''Go home! Leave me alone. Neither one of us has got the guts of a-a flea.''

''Let's prove you wrong,'' Travis said urgently. ''Let's take a risk. Both of us.''

''We're not going n-near my bedroom.''

''I'm not suggesting we do. I've got to get out of town, Julie. Breathe some clean salt air, try to get my sense of proportion back. My friend Bryce offered me his cottage for the weekend. Come with me, you can have your own room if that's what it takes. I just want to be with you by the ocean. That's all.''

''That's a lot,'' said Julie.

''If I spend one more day cooped up in that bloody condo, I'll go out of my mind.''

''I understand the feeling,'' she said with a small smile.

''I dare you to come with me.''

If she didn't want to end up like her mother, she didn't want to be alone like Leonora, either. Wasn't sitting in her apartment all weekend on a par with Pearl's behavior? Besides, she was still feeling deathly tired, a symptom she was doing her best to ignore. A weekend by the sea was just what she needed; it would also take her mind off the fact that her period was now two days later than it had been on Wednesday.

She wasn't pregnant. She couldn't be. She didn't even want to consider the possibility with Travis sitting so treacherously close to her. "I never could refuse a dare," she said.

"Go pack," Travis ordered.

His smile made him look ten years younger, Julie thought humbly. She got up, washed her face in the bathroom, threw some clothes in a case and came back into the living room. "We'd better go. Before I change my mind."

Twenty minutes later, after Travis had also packed a bag for the weekend, they were on the road, driving north. Julie sat back, closing her eyes, and fell asleep with the suddenness of a child.

Travis drove on, stealing sideways looks at his companion. She'd lost weight, he thought. And the shadows under her eyes were new. He was almost sure he was the reason.

He had a weekend to persuade her that separate rooms was a very bad idea; and that after the weekend, he wanted to keep on seeing her. If he suggested they share a room, would that be another dare she couldn't refuse? The way her dark lashes lay on her cheeks and the soft curve of her mouth in sleep filled him with an emotion he could only call tenderness.

A brand-new emotion.

He couldn't be in love. He'd never fallen in love, not once. After his broken engagement, he'd had women through the years, of course he had. But he'd always been careful to caution them that romance, commitment and marriage weren't part of his vocabulary.

There'd been those who'd tried to change his mind. But they hadn't succeeded.

So what was different about Julie?

She hadn't liked the way he'd spoken to Leonora. To his

mother, Travis corrected himself inwardly. The two words felt strange, almost as though they had no connection to him. Why was he so angry with his mother, when his father had behaved even more reprehensibly? Leonora hadn't left home meaning never to return. It was Charles who'd ensured her absence would be permanent. Logically, it was Charles he should be angry with. However, logic didn't seem to have much to do with that constrained meeting in Leonora's apartment. He'd felt like a chunk of granite on the beach. And as cold as the waves of the sea.

He owed Leonora an apology, he supposed. He might even be able to have a civilized conversation with her at some point in the future. But how could he ever revive the instinctual love a child has for his mother? Hadn't that died, all those years ago? He and his mother were strangers to each other.

One thing he would do. He'd visit Charles very soon, and have it out with him. That would give him considerable satisfaction. As for Jenessa, once Leonora had contacted her, he'd phone and find out how she felt about this revelation.

Another thing he needed to do was visit Julie's parents. With or without her consent. Although he still didn't know if he was in love with Julie, less and less could he contemplate being without her. Whatever that meant.

The last three weeks had felt like three years.

The miles rolled by, the shadows lengthening across the road as it wound along the coastline. He started watching for the signpost that indicated Bryce's driveway. Yesterday, when he'd been almost sure he'd act on the invitation, he'd phoned the couple who kept an eye on the cottage for Bryce; by now, they'd have cleaned the place for him and stocked it with groceries. He was glad he'd done that. He didn't want to have to leave the cottage for something as mundane as groceries. He wanted to spend every minute of its peaceful seclusion with Julie.

When he turned off the highway a few minutes later, Julie woke up. "Are we there?" she mumbled.

"Just about."

He pulled up beside the cottage, letting the view speak for itself: a private beach, the curl of waves on the sand, a scattering of islands skirted with foam and then the open ocean. Nearer to hand, he and Julie were enclosed by tall pines and stands of young maple. A couple of times since Bryce had bought the property seven years ago, Travis had come here on vacation. It was, he supposed, as near to Manatuck as he could get.

Julie said softly, "How beautiful…"

"You are, yes," he said.

She flushed, ducking her head. Then she looked straight at him. "I don't want separate rooms. Do you?"

His heart leaped in his chest. "Nope."

"Well," she said with a grin, "that was easy. And even though I lust after you, Travis, I'm also very hungry. Is there anything to eat in this utterly marvelous place?"

"Besides you, there's a refrigerator full of groceries."

"Refrigerator first," she said. "Me afterward."

He captured her hands in his, smiling into her brilliant green eyes. "Promise?"

"You bet."

"If you're afraid of ending up like your mother," he said dryly, "I don't think you have a worry in the world."

"I don't want to talk about mothers. Yours or mine."

"What, no fights?"

"One of the things I like about you—apart from your body—is that you catch on fast."

"You know what?" Travis said huskily. "Right now I wouldn't change places with anyone in the world."

"Neither would I," she said, almost inaudibly.

Julie wouldn't say what she didn't mean. Feeling light-headed with happiness, Travis said, "Let's grab our stuff, raid the refrigerator and light the barbecue. Or else, dearest Julie, you're going to find yourself in the bedroom."

"Steak—or even a hamburger—takes precedence," she said primly, and scrambled out of the vehicle.

Travis got out, too. "Come here," he said.

She walked around the hood of his car, flung her arms around him and burrowed her cheek into his chest. "Okay. Now what?"

"Now this," said Travis, and kissed her with all the passion and skill he was capable of. When he finally raised his head, his heart was thumping as though he'd run the Boston Marathon. He said unevenly, "I won't need a match to light the barbecue."

"I don't care if it's hot dogs," she whispered.

"One of these days I'll have to thank Brent for inviting you to Manatuck."

Julie laughed. "I'm sure he'll be impressed."

"You and I wouldn't have met, otherwise."

"I'm glad we did," Julie said with sudden intensity.

"So am I," said Travis, and kissed her again.

Somehow this interchange set the tone for the next two days. He and Julie spent a good deal of that time in bed, although they also made love up against the pantry door and, rather uncomfortably, underneath a pine tree. They swam, cavorting in the chill waves. They washed dishes together, discussing the politics of dictatorship and the perils of guerilla warfare. They barbecued shrimp, smothered pancakes in fresh strawberries and cream, and hiked in the woods. Travis sang in the shower; Julie taught him a Tanzanian tribal dance. They laughed a lot.

When they were loading their bags into the car on Sunday evening, Travis put a hand on Julie's arm and said forcibly, "This weekend wasn't just about sex, Julie."

She glanced over at him. "No," she said uncertainly, "it wasn't."

"When will I see you again?"

"Thursday?"

"Not until then?"

"Monday I'm taking my mother to a movie that she wants to see and my father thinks isn't worth the price of admission. On Tuesday I'm meeting my friend Kathy after work—remember her, Andrea's mother? And every Wednesday I work late."

He quelled a flicker of unease. "I'll meet you at the clinic on Thursday around five-thirty?"

"That'd be fine." She took one last look around, adding with a touch of desperation, "I hate to leave here, Travis. I'm not ready for the real world."

"This is the real world. You and I together, there's nothing more real than that. Anyway, we can come back. Bryce won't be needing the cottage for a while."

She made an indeterminate sound and climbed into the car. Travis accelerated up the driveway. He'd purposely not suggested she stay at his place tonight. He'd rushed her last time; he wasn't planning on repeating that mistake. But he wanted her to stay. He wanted her to move in with him, he thought with a tiny lurch of surprise; even though he'd never lived with a woman in his life. More than that, he wanted some kind of commitment from her.

He was only here another three weeks, while her contract expired in the middle of September. Then what? She'd mentioned the possibility of going to a clinic in Thailand, while it looked more and more likely that he'd be heading off to Mexico.

Was that what she meant by the real world?

CHAPTER FIFTEEN

BY TEN o'clock the next morning, Julie had lost her breakfast twice over. Leaning on the basin in the washroom nearest to her office, she stared at her paper-white face in the mirror. The flu. It had to be the flu. It couldn't be morning sickness.

She splashed cold water on her face and went back to work. Apart from the tiredness that had been dogging her for a couple of weeks, she felt fine the rest of the day. The movie was about the mishaps of a family wedding and made both her and her mother laugh, a brief intimacy that felt very precious to Julie. That night she slept as soundly as a baby, cautiously ate a bowl of cereal the next morning and didn't even make it to the apartment door before she had to rush to the bathroom. Afterward, not giving herself time to think, she picked up the phone and was lucky enough to get an appointment with her doctor during her lunch hour the following day.

When she saw him, he only confirmed what Julie already, in her heart, knew to be true. She was pregnant.

She walked out of his office like a woman in a daze. If she had to be pregnant, why couldn't the father have been some shadowy, insubstantial character who'd fade into the wallpaper now that she'd conceived? But Travis wasn't like that. Travis was flesh and blood, all too real, with an incisive intelligence and a temper to go with it. It was difficult to imagine him fading into anything.

What was she going to do? She had a date with him tomorrow night. She had less than thirty hours to come up with an answer.

The baby wasn't the issue. It was quite clear to her, and had been ever since the doctor had pronounced the word *pregnant*, that she would have the baby and rearrange her life to take care of it. If she had to trade off her wandering work habits with a real, live baby, the baby won hands down. It was interesting, Julie thought slowly, what a visit to a doctor's office could teach you about yourself.

The problem wasn't the baby. The problem was Travis. She had to tell him. Didn't she?

Eventually, she thought. With a bit of luck, she wouldn't start to show until late September, by which time he'd be in Mexico. That gave her a few weeks' grace. She'd have to be utterly discreet about the morning sickness; she knew from experience how gossip flourished in clinics and hospitals, whether they were in Maine or Calcutta.

She'd start getting up earlier; get it over with before she even left her apartment.

Feeling slightly better for these decisions, Julie caught the bus back to work. On Thursday, despite her best intentions, she still felt very queasy when she arrived at the clinic. Her first appointment wasn't until nine-thirty. She'd catch up on some paperwork in the meantime.

She was compiling her monthly statistics when a tap came at her door. "Come in," she called, scowling down at her desk because two columns that were supposed to add up refused to do so.

"Good morning, Julie," Travis said jauntily.

Her jaw dropped. Travis. Right in front of her. Standing on the other side of her desk, dwarfing her tiny office. Sickness rose in her throat, her face suddenly cold and clammy. With all the willpower she possessed she tried to force the nausea down. "I'm not—" she began, then gasped, "Excuse me," and ran for the door, pushing past him as though he were a piece of furniture.

She made it to the bathroom just in time. Ten minutes

later, knowing she had no other choice, she went back to her office. "What's wrong?" Travis said tersely, his eyes fastened on her pale cheeks.

"I must have eaten something that disagreed with me," she said rapidly. "I feel better already, it's nothing. What are you doing here?"

He kicked the door shut behind him. "You're pregnant, aren't you?"

"I wish you'd stop saying that," she said peevishly. "Do we still have a date for tonight?"

"Julie, answer me. Are you or are you not pregnant?"

"Yes," she said, "I am."

"Then we'll get married as soon as we can."

"I—*what* did you say?"

"And we'll stay married. No child of mine is going to be abandoned the way I was."

"It's customary to ask a woman if she wants to get married. Not tell her."

"These are exceptional circumstances."

Her temper rose one more notch. "I don't want to get married. Don't take it personally, Travis, it wouldn't matter who you were. The answer's no."

"You don't get it, do you? You're not being given a choice. I'll get a special licence, probably for next week."

"You don't love me," Julie said in a stony voice.

"This isn't about love. Or romance. It's about a child who's going to have two parents. Not one."

"I had two parents who don't love each other. That's the worst thing you can do to a child!"

"I've never met your parents, but I'd be willing to bet that you're as different from your mother as you can be. And if I'm like your father, I'd be surprised."

"We're not in love—we can't get married," she said desperately.

"We mean something to each other, you know that as well as I do. We'll build on that, Julie."

"You're not listening to me!"

"I've been offered a plum position in a new hospital in Mexico, near Cuernavaca. They have a physio clinic, you could get a part-time position there."

"You've got to stop this—I won't marry you."

He said flatly, "There's something I haven't asked you, something very obvious. Do you hate the idea of being pregnant?"

"No, as a matter of fact, I don't," she said truthfully. "But as a single mother, Travis."

"That's out of the question."

"According to you."

"It's my child, too," he said with menacing softness.

"Why didn't we stop and *think* before we made love?"

"Because there's something elemental between us," he said ruthlessly, raising one hand and running it down the side of her face to the hollow at the base of her throat, where her pulse quickened in spite of herself. "Don't bother denying it."

"You can't base a marriage on passion!"

"There are a lot worse things to base it on." He frowned down at her. "I'll look into the licence this morning. Then I want to meet your parents. In the meantime, I'll call Bryce and see if he'll be best man. Who do you want to stand with you?"

"You're like an avalanche, carrying everything in its path," Julie said furiously. "What about your mother, will you invite her?"

His smile didn't reach his eyes. "That'd throw Charles into a tailspin. Although, the more I think about it, the more convinced I am that he already knows Leonora's in Portland, and he staged that fake reconciliation with me to get me away from her."

"Have you been in touch with her?" Julie persisted.

For the first time, Travis wouldn't meet her gaze. "Not yet, no."

"If you're to marry me," she taunted, "you'll have to, won't you?"

"There's no *if* about it, Julie."

He was standing altogether too close. She squeezed past him, putting her desk between them, and found the courage to ask the only meaningful question. "Why do you want to marry me, Travis?"

"I told you. Because of the child."

"Nothing to do with me, then."

"Come off it—you spent last weekend with me, you know how well we're matched."

She said with true despair, "But that won't last!"

"I disagree. But even if I didn't, do we lock ourselves in separate cages, stay alone for our entire lives? I don't think so."

Was that why she wanted the baby, Julie wondered with uncomfortable honesty. So she wouldn't be alone? She wanted the baby, but not the baby's father.

As though he'd read her mind, Travis said abruptly, "Were you going to tell me you were pregnant?"

"I only found out yesterday."

In a voice like a knife blade, he repeated, "Were you going to tell me?"

"Yes," she said dully, "eventually."

"When it suited you. After I'd left Portland."

She lowered her eyes, ashamed. Put like that, her plan sounded shoddy and underhanded. "I haven't had much time to think," she said defensively.

"Nor are you going to," he said grimly. "I'll let you know the date of the wedding as soon as I've looked after the legalities. Tonight we'll go and see your parents."

"Oh, no, we won't," she flared. "If this travesty of a

marriage is to take place, I'm going to see them first. By myself. To break the news.''

''Then we'll go together tomorrow night.''

The force of his willpower beat against her, as pitiless as the surf on the ocean. A cliff might seem impregnable, she thought, but the water's ceaseless pounding would eventually topple it. ''You're taking for granted that I'll marry you.''

He smiled crookedly. ''I dare you to marry me.''

She didn't smile back. ''I don't like being taken for granted.''

He suddenly pounded his fist on her desk, making her jump. ''This is all wrong, the way we're going about this! Remember the weekend, Julie. I don't know if I love you. I always figured I didn't know how to love a woman, I'd lost that capacity when my mother disappeared. But I'm sure not indifferent to you, nor you to me. Give us a chance, that's all I ask. Look how we laughed and made love and talked all weekend…I'm more real with you than I've ever been in my life.''

She stared up at him, shaken. She couldn't fault him for honesty, she thought, and sought for an answering honesty in herself. ''To marry you…it frightens me more than I can say.''

He closed the distance between them, reaching out for her. But Julie shrank from him, knowing if he so much as laid a finger on her she'd weep as though her heart was broken. Travis stopped dead in his tracks, a flash of pure agony lacerating the deep blue of his eyes. But then it was gone, leaving her to wonder if she'd imagined it. He said coldly, ''I'll call you later in the day.''

As he wheeled and left her office, she made a tiny, instinctive gesture toward him. But he was striding away from her and didn't see it. Reaching for her chair like a blind woman, Julie sat down. Travis disappeared around a corner.

The man who wanted to marry her. Because she was pregnant.

In her lunch hour Julie phoned Leonora, asking if she could come and see her right after work. So at five forty-five, Julie was walking into Leonora's cool, austere living room. It was interesting, she thought numbly, that it was to Travis's mother, not her own, that she'd come for help. She said, "I have to talk to you."

Leonora sat down in a graceful flow of movement. "Is it about Travis?"

"Yes." Absently Julie tugged at a loose thread in her uniform. "I wasn't wholly truthful with you about Travis and me."

"I'd wondered," Leonora said mildly.

"Until I met him, I'd only slept with one other man, back in my college days. My parents' marriage is a disaster, and I'd long ago decided marriage and commitment weren't for me." Warm color crept up her cheeks. "And then I met Travis, and I just about dragged him into my bed. Not that he was unwilling," she added hastily.

"I'm sure he wasn't."

"We have these huge fights all the time. We spent last weekend together and it was wonderful and then on Wednesday I found out I was pregnant."

For the first time, Leonora was taken aback. "Julie..."

"Travis dropped in to see me at my office this morning. I have this awful morning sickness and he guessed right away. He insists we're to get married immediately. Leonora, I can't marry him! We don't love each other."

"If you don't marry him, what will you do?"

"Have the baby. Find a job somewhere in the States and settle down."

"On your own."

Julie raised her chin. "What's wrong with that?"

"And where does the baby's father fit into this picture?"

"I don't know! I guess he'd visit sometimes."

"Julie, I've only seen Travis as an adult that one evening here in my apartment, but I can't imagine he'd be satisfied with so peripheral a role. He would at least demand joint custody."

"But—"

"You'd be tied to him for the next seventeen or eighteen years. Why not marry him? There's obviously something very powerful between you."

"Sex," Julie said in an unfriendly voice.

"I'd call it passion."

"I thought you'd be on my side!"

"This is my grandchild, Julie—or had you forgotten that?"

She had. Julie buried her head in her hands. "Ever since I met Travis, I haven't been able to think straight," she wailed. "I had my life under control. Lots of adventure and travel, work I love, and no ties. I wish I'd never met him!"

"But you have," Leonora said reasonably. "Travis was abandoned as a child. Do you seriously think he'll abandon his own child?"

"Then what am I to do?"

"Marry him. I'm not saying you'll have a peaceful, uneventful life, you're both too strong-minded for that. Too independent. However, if you're willing, I think you might find love with Travis. But only if you're willing, Julie."

Julie bit her lip. She'd come running to Leonora for sympathy and for comfort. But Leonora's standards were far too stringent to offer anything easy or sentimental. So she, Julie, was once again being forced back on herself.

"Travis is behaving abominably toward you," she said.

"He isn't ready yet," Leonora said with painful truth.

"And no, my suggestion that you marry him isn't to further my own cause. I wouldn't do that to you."

Julie pushed herself to her feet. "You're an amazing woman, Leonora. In all this mess, one thing's clear—I'd be delighted to have you as a mother-in-law."

Leonora smiled, giving Julie a brief hug. "That's very sweet of you. In my heart of hearts, I'm convinced you're made for each other, you and Travis. That's easy for me to say but not as easy for you to hear."

"You'd be invited to the wedding. If there is one."

"I'll attend. When it happens."

"You're very like Travis," Julie said darkly. "I'll talk to you soon. 'Bye."

She hurried home to her apartment. When she got in the door, the phone was ringing. Picking it up as if it were something loathsome she'd found under a rock, she said, "Hello?"

"Travis here. We're on for Sunday afternoon, three o'clock at St. Margaret's. I'll let Charles and Leonora know, as well as Brent and Jenessa. I talked to Bryce and he'll fly in on Saturday."

Her heart jouncing in her chest, Julie said, "You're taking my consent for granted."

"You'll see your parents tonight. Don't forget I want to meet them tomorrow night. You and I can go for dinner first, I'll pick you up at six-thirty."

He sounded as impersonal as if he were a booking agent, she thought with a spurt of fury. "Yes, sir."

"I've gotten a substitute for my medical practice from Monday until Thursday. I called the clinic and they're willing to give you three days off. So we'll go back to the resort. I was able to get the same cottage."

"You're treating me like a cipher!"

There was a taut silence. "What kind of flowers do you like?"

"Anything but roses. I've always hated clichés."

"This wedding will be as far from a cliché as it can get," he said. "Let me tell you something, Julie, and then I'm going to hang up. When I thought of settling in Mexico while you took off to Thailand, I didn't know how I was going to stand it."

And just what did he mean by that? Abruptly Julie realized she was holding a receiver that was humming in her ear. Damn him anyway, she thought, and banged it back in its holder. Flowers, church, a best man and a honeymoon: they were nothing but window-dressing.

Yet somehow, tacitly, she seemed to have agreed to this travesty of a wedding.

She threw together a salad, then went to see her parents to tell them she was getting married. Predictably, her mother turned misty-eyed and sentimental, while her father asked some very pointed questions about Travis's financial state. Neither thought to ask if she was happy. But as she got up to leave, her father said suspiciously, "It's all very sudden, Julie. Is this a shotgun wedding?"

"Really, Thomas, how crude of you, of course Julie wouldn't do anything like that," Pearl said, and smiled at her daughter. "We haven't asked you what you'd like for a wedding present, darling."

Like a tidal wave and just as unstoppable, Julie was suddenly overwhelmed with rage. She closed her eyes and counted to ten. It didn't help. White-faced, she said in a clipped voice, "You know what I'd like? I'd like you two to go to a marriage counsellor or else get a divorce. One or the other."

"*Julie!*"

For once they'd spoken in unison. But not even this minor miracle could deflect Julie. "Why do you think I've scarcely had a boyfriend, let alone contemplated marriage? Because my parents put me off love and marriage by the time I was five. You won't have an honest fight, will you? You'd rather make digs at each other all day long, never resolve anything, live like enemies under the same roof. Yes, I'm pregnant. Pregnant and terrified that I'll end up like you.''

"I won't tolerate you speaking to us like this," Thomas snapped.

"It's too late, Dad—I already have. And you know what?" Julie added with an incredulous laugh. "It feels great. Let me tell you something else. As a little girl, I always thought it must be my fault—that I was the reason you didn't get along. But I'm not going to think that way anymore. You were adults. You were responsible."

"That's not—" Pearl sputtered.

Julie swept on. "One more thing before I leave. I want both of you to go upstairs to the attic, look in the box with all the albums in it, and take out your wedding photo. Take ten minutes to sit there and look at it. See if you recognize yourselves...I sure didn't." She grabbed her purse. "I'll see you tomorrow evening. Good night."

She ran down the steps and marched along the sidewalk. But once she was out of sight of the prim little bungalow where she'd grown up, Julie took a detour into a small park near the elementary school. Sinking down on an empty bench, she realized her hands were trembling like leaves in the wind. She rested them on her knees, watching them impersonally, as if they didn't belong to her. Would her parents go up to the attic? Or would they, as usual, bury her request in a barrage of mutual recrimination?

She didn't know. Oh, Travis, she thought, staring blindly at the gravel path, what are we doing?

CHAPTER SIXTEEN

PROMPTLY at six-thirty on Friday evening, Travis drew up outside Julie's apartment. Inside, the little red-headed boy he remembered from his first visit was bicycling up and down the hallway, banging into the walls with indiscriminate enthusiasm. Travis pushed the buzzer, restlessly moving his shoulders while he waited. He'd been behaving atrociously, giving Julie orders, refusing to consult her in any of the decisions about the wedding; he couldn't seem to help himself. He must try to apologize tonight. If she'd let him.

Once they were safely married, the ring on her finger, he'd relax. They'd have three days together beside the ocean, in the cottage with the big bed. They'd be fine.

Impatiently he pushed the buzzer again. Perhaps she'd been late from work and was still in the shower. He'd like to surprise her wet and naked, he thought, desire like an ache in his belly.

A couple had entered the building behind him; the man held the security door open for him. "Thanks," Travis said briefly, and took the stairs two at a time. But when he knocked on Julie's door, there was no answer. He stood still, straining to hear any sounds through the wood.

Only silence. He knocked again, louder, visited by the unpleasant certainty that she wasn't there. The apartment was empty.

The ache in his gut was no longer desire, but fear. He waited another few minutes before knocking again, again without a response. Then he ran downstairs. He hadn't gone to his condo after work; maybe there was a message there for him.

Fear transformed itself into terror. She was in the early stages of pregnancy. Surely she was all right?

As he lunged for the door, the little boy said, "She went away."

Travis turned. "Who?"

"The lady with the green eyes."

"What do you mean, she went away?"

"After lunch she came downstairs with a suitcase and got in a red car and drove away."

"Do you know where she went?" Travis croaked.

"I didn't ask. My mother says it's rude to ask people too many questions," he said virtuously.

Wishing the boy's mother a thousand miles away, Travis said, "Thanks for telling me."

"She didn't even smile at me. Perhaps she's mad at me."

"I don't think she's very happy right now," Travis heard himself say. "She's not mad at you."

The boy gave him a gap-toothed grin, hauled his bicycle around in a circle and pedaled fast toward the end wall. Travis let himself out, wincing at the thunk of rubber against plaster. When he got to his condo, there was no note from Julie among his mail; but his answering machine was blinking. Steeling himself, he entered his password.

"Travis, this is Julie. I—I'm really sorry, but I can't go through with this. The wedding, I mean. I've rented a car and I'm going away for a few days, please don't try to follow me. I need to be alone to think. I just don't know what to *do*, ever since I met you my life's been out of control...I'll be in touch sometime next week. I—good-bye."

His first reaction was relief that she hadn't had a miscarriage; his second, fury that she could run away. But how could he blame her for not being able to think? He hadn't been behaving very rationally the last couple of days.

How about the last couple of months?

He poured himself a beer and stood by the window, watching one of the island ferries pull away from the dock. He had no idea where she'd gone. Even if he did, she didn't want him following her. So was he going to placidly sit home and wait for her to phone?

It was too late to reach Bryce and tell him not to come. How was he going to face his best friend? And what was the point in having a best man if there wasn't to be a wedding?

He knew what his third reaction was. He just didn't want to admit it. Pain, pure and simple. Julie had turned him down. Worse, she'd run away from him.

What other choice had he given her? What room to negotiate? None. No, he'd been too busy playing the macho, masterful male.

He slathered peanut butter on a thick wedge of bread and munched it standing by the window. Comfort food, he thought. Sticks to your ribs and the roof of your mouth. He washed the sandwich down with the last of his beer, cleaned his teeth, looked up an address in the phone book and left the condo.

The woman who answered the door of an obsessively neat bungalow bore almost no resemblance to Julie. He said politely, "Mrs. Renshaw? I'm Travis Strathern, Julie's fiancé. Is she here by any chance?"

"She's supposed to be with you."

"May I come in?"

The living room was tidy, bland and excruciatingly clean, as different from Julie's warm, eclectically decorated space as it could be. Then a man walked into the room. Dessicated, thought Travis, and introduced himself. He said, sitting down without an invitation, "Julie's run away

It's largely my fault, I haven't handled things well the last few days. Do you have any idea where she might have gone?''

"Run away?'' Pearl squeaked.

"She's pregnant,'' Thomas said accusingly.

"Yes. Does she have a favorite haunt she might have gone to?''

"If she did, we wouldn't know about it,'' Pearl said, twisting her fingers in her lap. "Julie was always a very private child.''

"Nonsense, Pearl.''

"It's not, Thomas. We were too busy arguing to pay her much attention.''

Thomas puffed up like a bantam rooster. "Must you discuss our private lives in front of a stranger?''

"He's not a stranger. He's the man who wants to marry Julie and he's the father of our grandchild,'' Pearl announced, then sat down hard on a puce wing chair, looking astounded at her own effrontery.

Despite the confusion of emotion in his chest, Travis was intrigued. He said intuitively, "Did Julie come to see you last night?''

Pearl looked at Thomas, who looked at Pearl. Neither seemed prepared to answer him, so Travis added carefully, "Julie's very afraid of marriage. She seems to think that love doesn't last. That it can't.''

"Ridiculous,'' Thomas snorted.

"We've ruined her life,'' Pearl wailed.

Travis said forcefully, "Your daughter is the only woman I've ever met with whom I want to spend the rest of my life. Yes, she's pregnant, but that isn't why I want to marry her. She stands up for herself, she loves adventure, she's intelligent and capable.'' He broke off with an impatient gesture. "Hell, I sound like I'm writing a resumé. She's also so beautiful she cuts me to the heart.''

Pearl quavered, "Thomas, you used to tell me how beautiful I was. A long time ago."

Thomas looked at her across the room. His voice creaking like a hinge that needed oiling, he said, "You still are, Pearl."

As Pearl blushed like a young bride, Travis saw the first fleeting resemblance to her daughter. He had no idea what was going on, although he sensed it was cataclysmic. Before he could think what to say next, Pearl blurted, "Julie was very angry with us last night. So this afternoon, Thomas and I phoned a marriage counsellor. Our first appointment is next week."

Julie must have been angry, Travis thought, smothering a smile. "That's a big step," he said in his best bedside manner.

"All this therapy stuff, don't know what good it does," Thomas huffed.

"We're going to find out," Pearl said. "Julie gave us an ultimatum, Mr. Strathern. She was really extremely angry." And she gave a small, secret smile.

Thomas had better watch out, thought Travis with another inner quiver of amusement, and got up to leave. "So neither of you has any idea where Julie might have gone?"

"Give us your phone number, and if we hear from her we'll contact you," Thomas suggested.

This was a huge endorsement. Travis did so, and took his leave. His next stop, he'd already decided, was Leonora's. He'd arrive without warning and take the risk that she wasn't home. But when he pressed her intercom, she answered, the connection so poor he couldn't tell if she was pleased to hear from him or not. Again, he took the stairs two at a time. He'd be in shape for his wedding, he thought wryly. If there ever was one.

"Hello, Travis," Leonora said.

She was wearing a slim-fitting denim skirt and a white

sweater, her hair pulled back with a vivid scarlet scarf. She looked both wary and pleased to see him. He walked into the living room and stood by the window, his back to the light. "Julie and I were to have been married on Sunday," he said. "But she's run away. Do you know where she is?"

"No. She was here yesterday afternoon. She's very afraid of commitment. And of her own feelings."

"She went to see her parents yesterday and read the riot act to them." He smiled at the tall, elegant woman who was his mother. "I'd like to have been there."

"Step one, anger. Step two, forgiveness," Leonora said.

"Are you applying that to me as well?"

"I know you're angry with me. And rightly so."

He said in frustration, "My mother died. I'm having trouble bringing her—you—back to life."

"I do understand." For a moment Leonora's voice faltered. "I only hope it's something you want to do."

"You're very direct."

"As are you. Julie, I'm sure, would agree with me."

"I've handled this fiasco of a wedding like a bull in a china shop."

"More like a herd of elephants in a glass factory," she said. "Did you give her an engagement ring?"

"No! It isn't that kind of wedding."

"What kind is it? You're engaged to be married, aren't you?"

"You're making me feel like a four-year-old caught with his hand in the cookie jar."

"You're in love with her, you know that."

"I lust after her and I like her," Travis said vigorously. "I don't call that love."

"In your way, you're as afraid of love as Julie is, that's why you've hounded her into this wedding. But riding roughshod over her isn't the way to win her." Leonora hesitated. "I'm always nervous about handing out advice. But as a young woman I turned my back on the love of my children to pursue my career as a dancer. That decision came at an extraordinarily high cost, Travis. In the long run, love is all we have."

"Do you regret being a dancer?"

"No. But if I'd been wiser, I might have been able to have dancing and my children."

"Charles might never have allowed that."

"Maybe." She gave a restless shrug. "Enough of the past. If I knew where Julie was, I'd tell you."

"You would, wouldn't you?" Impulsively he added, "Do you have any videos or film clips of your dancing?" As she nodded, he went on, "I'd like to borrow them. Soon."

"I'd be delighted to lend them to you."

He said slowly, "You'll never beg for my attention, will you?"

"Proud. Stiff-necked. I've been called both," she admitted. "No doubt you've inherited some of my less admirable characteristics as well as my best."

"Just ask Julie," he responded with a wry grin. Then he sobered. "I'm going to be in Portland for at least three more weeks. Will you stay here that long?"

"I'll stay as long as you want me to," Leonora said.

"I'm glad," Travis replied, and watched tears tremble on her lashes. Rare tears, he'd be willing to bet, and without even thinking about it crossed the carpet and hugged her.

She felt slight in his arms. Very briefly she rested her forehead on his shoulder. Then she moved back. "I never stopped loving you, Travis. You're always welcome to come and see me. You and Julie."

"I don't even know where to look for her!"

"She won't vanish off the face of the earth. She'll come back, you'll see."